THE QUEST FOR THE COLUMN

A RAT'S TALE

Peter Collins was born in London in 1968 and moved to Swindon at the age of six, where he still lives.

He has done various jobs and still works, but prefers the time he spends writing.

Peter Collins

THE QUEST FOR THE COLUMN

A RAT'S TALE

Olympia Publishers
London

www.olympiapublishers.com
OLYMPIA PAPERBACK EDITION

A CIP catalogue record for this title is
available from the British Library.

ISBN: 978-1-84897-218-6

This is a work of fiction.
Names, characters, places and incidents originate from the writer's
imagination. Any resemblance to actual persons, living or dead, is purely
coincidental.

First Published in 2012

Olympia Publishers
60 Cannon Street
London
EC4N 6NP

Printed in Great Britain

To Andrei, for reading my stories and of course to my Fruitcake x

Wednesday- A Little bit of Shopping

The sewers are a dark, damp and gloomy place and often they are quite smelly with horrible things floating in the dirty water. The sewers are also usually quite cold. Chilly, smelly air and dirty water make these many underground pipes leading from drains and toilets the kind of place no person would choose to enter. It is not unfair to say that these are not welcoming places to stay or even visit.

Though sewers are not the sort of place any sensible person would choose to live, small voices, squeaks even can sometimes be heard...

But now deep within the darkness of one of these tunnels a gentle rhythmic creaking and splashing can be heard. Something somewhere on the murky water is making a noise. Slowly the sounds grow steadily louder and clearer until eventually from out of the gloom a shape can be seen emerging.

Very slowly the shape grows clearer while the gentle creaking and splashing sounds grow louder as it approaches, until finally the gloom reveals a boat.

Gently floating in the murky water within the sewer is a little makeshift wooden rowing boat complete with oars.

The little rowing boat was once a novelty boat-shaped fruit bowl and the wooden spoons causing the splashing are serving very well as a pair of oars. Being so gloomy down here the little boat has a tiny stub of candle glowing on the front of the boat giving just a little bit of light in the darkness.

Sitting inside the boat are two rats, these are Roger and Brian and they are good friends. Roger and Brian have been spending the morning finding food and anything else they might need that has been thrown away by people; now they are on their way back home.

The two friends always row their little boat around in the sewers, but to them this network of tunnels is known as the Rats Underground, or simply called the R.U.

Even though it is cold, dark and smelly the Rats Underground is hugely popular with rats. Whether they walk along its dry banks or are lucky enough to own a boat like Roger and Brian who float around at leisure, the R.U. is often quite busy with rats travelling somewhere.

Roger is rowing the boat, he often rows the boat, while his friend happily sits relaxing and watching as the scenery of the tunnels slowly changes. Despite his love of rowing Roger is quite a chubby brown rat. Underneath his pale brown cords and pale blue T-shirt with RAT in large dark blue letters on the front, Roger is covered in brown fur, except for his long pink tail. A rat's tail is always long and hairless, including Roger's, which hangs behind him as he rows the boat. Beside Roger is his favourite baggy red sweatshirt that he always wears whenever he is cold but rowing the boat makes him quite warm so it rests beside him until he needs it again.

Opposite Roger in their boat is his good friend Brian. Unlike Roger, Brian is quite slim, thin even. Also unlike Roger who is a brown rat, Brian is a hooded rat, so beneath his pale blue jeans and dark blue hooded top Brian is covered in white fur. Except of course for his long pink tail, and a mop of black fur on the top of his head. In a white circle on the left of his hooded top are the white letters NYR, this, according to Brian, stands for New York Rats. Why rats in New York deserve a special mention on clothing Brian does not know and since he is just sitting in the boat idly fiddling with his tail it is probably fair to say that he does not really care. Instead just like Roger he is more concerned with getting their shopping home, between them on the floor of their boat they are almost buried in food and other things found that they might find useful. They are surrounded by nuts, seeds, bits of bread, pieces of fruit, broken biscuits and tea bags. Roger and Brian do enjoy drinking a nice hot cup of tea. So full is their little boat that neither can see their hairy bare feet in the bottom of the boat, they even have an old used box of matches using up what little space they have left.

'What do we need a used box of matches for anyway, Rog?' asks Brian.

'Well... I don't really know yet, to be honest,' admits Roger.

'They won't light, not a second time.' Brian observes.

'True, but I just thought they might prove useful.'

'You mean safety matches because they won't catch fire?' Brian asks with sarcasm.

'No,' replies Roger moodily, 'But we might find a use for second hand used matches that no longer strike and burn.' he adds vaguely.

'Oh well, we might find a use for them.' concedes Brian.

Rats are very clever little creatures and though they have never been known to build a city or put a rat on the moon they are still very good at solving problems. Right now Roger has the minor problem of proving that an old used box of matches is useful, otherwise he might appear to be daft.

'It's a box of wood, we can at least gnaw on them!' Roger answers winningly.

'Oh yeah, good idea!'

Rats, like all rodents, need to gnaw on something to prevent their constantly growing teeth from getting too long.

Creak, slosh, creak, slosh. Gently Roger keeps rowing the boat towards their home.

Creak, slosh, creak, slosh.

Home for Roger and Brian is a storm drain in a quiet street with nice new houses close to the football ground and not too far from the town centre. A storm drain is an open grate in the gutter next to the kerb which allows rain water to drain away. This however makes their home a cold, draughty and damp place to live but Roger and Brian do not mind this too much, despite these problems they have made their home quite cosy.

Once they reach home Roger and Brian tie their boat up nice and secure in the R.U. Grabbing some bits of shopping from their boat they walk upwards through the narrow pipe which leads into the storm drain which they happily call home.

'Home again, Rog,' Brian sighs.

'At last, I'm looking forward to a lazy couple of days. Rest and do nothing, that's my plan,' Roger says yawning.

'Yeah, a nice long rest, I like the sound of that, it'll be like a holiday.' Brian agrees.

Roger and Brian make a few trips up and down the pipe getting all the food from their boat and stored away nicely into their home.

Finally Brian returns from the boat carrying the old used box of matches, he holds them waiting for Roger to say something. Roger keeps quiet, he does not say a word, he knows his friend still sees no use for them.

'We've already got a nice big matchbox with four matches as legs.' Brian observes.

'Yeah, we call it the table. And there are four wooden blocks for chairs,' Roger observes quickly.

'Yeah... um.'

'Which means we might find a good use for this matchbox!' Roger says triumphantly.

Roger and Brian have a well furnished home, they both even have beds, these were once the little plastic tubs takeaway food is delivered in, now they are lined with hankies for warmth and comfort. Being rats they would much prefer woodchips but living in a damp storm drain this would not be practical

Despite being cold, damp and draughty Roger and Brian really like their home in the storm drain. One reason for this is because it is so close to the Rats Underground.

This network of tunnels is popular with many rats, not only because down here they are safe from dangers such as dogs but for the very simple reason that down here on the R.U they can safely and easily travel anywhere.

Roger and Brian have now finished putting their shopping away so they settle down with a nice hot cup of tea. The two friends often enjoy drinking tea, whenever they can or whenever they have been working hard.

'It's been a busy week, Brian, and it's only Wednesday,' Roger notes.

'Yeah, I'm tired already,' admits Brian.

'Yeah we've had work on the R.U. and we had to help my mum yesterday,' Roger adds.

'Yeah, I hate Mondays, I've never enjoyed clearing out them tunnels. It's too dirty,' complains Brian.

'Just because we live on the R.U. we have to clear them out. Yuk! Not right that, many rats use the R.U.,' moans Roger.

After a pause to drink tea the two friends sit silently in thought for a moment, they are both so glad just to be resting.

'We were busy yesterday as well, Brian,' Roger says between slurps.

'I don't mind helping your mum, Rog, she always feeds us,' Brian replies happily.

'True. I don't know where she finds all that food, my mum shops better than us,' Roger admits.

Again the two friends fall silent and return to drinking their hot tea from their thimbles, they are both feeling tired today.

'Do you know what I'd like to do tonight Rog?' asks Brian.

'Nothing I hope,' replies Roger.

'I tell you what I'd like to do,' Brian begins, 'I'd like to relax, put my feet up, clean my tail and stare over my hairy toes.'

'That's a relief, I thought you were planning on being busy,' admits Roger.

'No, too tired, I also want a nice long lie-in tomorrow.'

'Good, me too! Tonight I'm going to sit and read my paper,' Roger decides.

It is much later in the evening now and the two friends are happily carrying out the plans they had earlier promised themselves: Brian is lying on his bed staring over his hairy toes relaxing while Roger is sitting at their matchbox table reading his tatty newspaper. Though it being dark, Roger manages to read by the light of the streetlamp above their storm drain. The light comes through the gaps in the grating of the storm drain, Roger, though sits to one side rather than right below. This is just as well as tonight it is pouring with rain and living beneath a gutter in the road, water gushes through past them. Brian relaxes listening to the gurgling sounds of the water running into the Rats Underground beyond their home. Brian is more relaxed than Roger, he is tucked up nice and cosy in bed, with water falling close to where Roger is sitting; it is cold and damp.

'It's cold tonight Brian,' says Roger.

'It's warm where I am,' replies Brian, cheekily.

Roger looks at his own bed and realises that it is cold enough to see his own breath. He wants to sit and read his paper for a while longer but the cold is making him feel very uncomfortable, even his paws are beginning to feel stiff with the cold. Reluctantly, Roger gives up reading and climbs into his own bed where he soon feels reasonably warm.

'Ah that's better, anyway I can finish reading my paper tomorrow,' Roger sighs.

'Yeah, it's a nice easy day tomorrow. Now we might as well just listen to the rain pouring,' suggests Brian.

'Yeah, might as well, it's quite relaxing really,' admits Roger.

The two friends lay down in their beds; takeaway food tubs with hankies for blankets make decent beds and they are both warm and cosy. Listening to the rain pattering in the gutter above them, dripping past them through their home and gurgling as it runs down into the Rats Underground is quite soothing. They are fairly safe as the water is running away and not flooding so they stay in bed and relax. They also feel safe in the knowledge that they can fall asleep and wake up whenever they are ready to wake up and the two friends can lie in as long as they wish. They can even choose to miss breakfast.

Thursday – An Alarming Start

The sun has risen but Roger and Brian have not. The sun is up and shining brightly through the occasional patch of little fluffy white cloud in an otherwise clear blue sky, yet the two friends are still in a deep sleep. The sun's light and its warmth beams down through the grating into their storm drain home. Such a nice day is usually enough to wake anyone wishing to make the most of good weather, but not Roger and Brian, they still sleep. Even the merry singing of the birds in the trees does not manage to wake them.

But if there is one thing that is likely to wake the two friends from their slumbers then it is likely to be the Rats Underground Herald who is standing in their storm drain home.

A Herald is a messenger and he can easily be recognised by the bright red tabard he is wearing, this is like a sleeveless jacket or vest. On the Herald's tabard is the usual R.U. emblem over the wearer's heart, a yellow R with a yellow U below and slightly to the right within a blue circle. But just in case a Herald wearing a bright red tabard with the R.U emblem is not clear enough it has a big stern yellow H on the front and back.

A herald is good at delivering messages and a uniform or at least tabard is good at letting you know who is delivering the message but to receive a message it helps to be awake. The Herald also carries a bell and seeing that both Roger and Brian are fast asleep he decides to wake them with the use of his bell.

Ding!

Dong!

Ding!

Dong!!!

The Herald happily rings his bell loudly, the clanging sound is deafening, understandably this quickly wakes the two friends up from their deep restful sleep.

'Did you order an alarm call?' Roger asks Brian.

'No, not me,' answers Brian.

'Me neither,' adds Roger.

On confirming this both friends roll over in their beds and attempt to go back to sleep, sadly this simply will not be allowed to happen. Realising this the Herald simply rings his bell again only this time with much more effort.

Ding dong!

Ding dong!

Ding dong!

Ding dong ding dong ding doooonnngggg!!!!!!!!

Brian pokes his head out from his bed and turns to his tired friend.

'He's not going to go away, is he, Rog?'

'No, I don't think he is and I don't think he will even if we ask him,' notes Roger.

'No, he seems stubborn to me,' observes Brian.

'He seems annoying to me,' admits Roger.

Reluctantly the two friends accept that their nice long lie-in has now officially ended, worse still they suspect they are wanted for some reason.

Finally deciding that he has their attention the Herald puts down his bell and reaches inside his tabard. He pulls out a great rolled up sheet of paper and prepares to deliver his message.

'I have a summons for you,' explains the Herald.

'Who are you?' asks Brian.

'I'm Gerald,' answers the Herald.

'And what are you?' asks Roger.

'I'm, a Herald,' he answers proudly.

'Gerald, the Herald?' responds Roger.

'What's a Herald?' asks Brian.

'It's a messenger,' Roger answers quietly.

'Oh, I see.'

'Do you mind if I deliver my message?' asks the Herald, with impatience.

'Go on, herald away,' offers Brian.

The Herald unrolls his sheet of paper and clears his throat preparing to speak.

'A summons?' the two friends suddenly say.

The two friends look nervously at each other, they have never had a summons before, no one has ever demanded they appear anywhere, they begin to wonder what they might have done wrong.

"You are both summoned by Jeremy Brown, Chair-rat of the Rats Underground Southwest Drains Region to appear at his desk in his office at Hastings House by midday today," the Herald reads.

'Why, what have we done?' asks Brian.

'Or what haven't we done?' asks Roger.

'I don't know,' replies the Herald.

'Why not?' demands Brian.

'All I know is what it says here,' answers the Herald.

'And how to ring a bell,' Roger notes.

'Loudly,' adds Brian.

'Very loudly,' Roger agrees.

'Well you wouldn't have listened if you weren't awake,' the Herald replies.

'True,' admits Roger.

'Which is why I rang my bell,' Gerald the Herald explains.

'Yeah, but you didn't have to enjoy it so much. I nearly jumped out of my bed,' complains Brian.

His words are unfortunately wasted, Gerald the Herald has already turned and walked out of their storm drain home. He is now below entering the Rats Underground and heading back to Hastings House where he will announce that the message has been received. As they live and work on the Rats Underground the Herald knows Roger and Brian are wise enough to follow such an order, this is why he did not wait for a reply or return with them.

Instead Roger and Brian are left sitting up in their beds knowing that somehow today is not going to be the nice lazy day they had planned.

'Oh well, business as usual,' sighs Roger.

'Yeah... At least it's a nice day,' Brian notices.

They look up through the grating to see that last night's heavy rain has gone and now the sun is shining brightly.

'Oh yeah, so it is,' Roger sees.

'Pity really, we'll have to travel on the R.U. to Hastings House,' Brian says.

'As I said, business as usual,' adds Roger.

After a very late breakfast Roger and Brian slowly plod their way down to where their little rowing boat is moored on the R.U. This is easy enough to reach, it is simply at the end of the pipe that joins their storm drain home to the main sewer that they know as the R.U. so it is just a very short walk.

'Rog, do you think we're in trouble?' Brian asks nervously.

'I shouldn't think so. We've not done anything wrong, or badly,' replies Roger soothingly.

'True. But what we think is a good job others sometimes think is terrible,' Brian observes.

'Only sometimes Brian. Anyway, we know when we've done well or not,' assures Roger wisely.

Once they reach their boat on the Rats Underground the two friends untie it from its moorings and climb aboard. Now they can begin their journey to Hastings House and, as usual, Roger takes the oars and starts rowing.

Hastings House is where Jeremy Brown Chair-rat of the Rats Underground Southwest Drains Region has his head office. Hastings House also happens to be right beneath the bus drivers' canteen at the bus station, so naturally this is a busy place where both people and rats do a lot of travelling. Now Roger and Brian are heading that way.

'Well what do you think we're wanted for then?' asks Brian.

'I don't know,' admits Roger.

'I mean we've always worked hard, haven't we?'

'Yeah, we have,' agrees Roger.

'And we've worked a lot for the R.U. haven't we Rog?'

'We have, yeah,' agrees Roger, adding after a thought 'Maybe that's it.'

'Maybe what?' asks Brian.

'Well after all the work we've done maybe they're going to reward us,' suggests Roger, hopefully.

'Yeah!' Brian responds excitedly, 'And maybe Jeremy Brown, the Chair-rat himself is going to give us an award or something,' he adds.

'It's possible,' Roger adds quietly.

'I wonder what we will get?' Brian asks.

So now with this wonderful thought in mind Roger and Brian with less nerves and growing excitement make their way towards Hastings House to see the Chair-rat.

Roger and Brian live close to the football ground which is near the town centre, fortunately this means they do not need to travel very far. Rowing gently the two friends leave the quiet stretch of tunnel that leads from their own street onto a wider and more busy part of the Rats Underground. Now they are entering the R.U where rats are often travelling back and forth, here rats are on the move many hours of the day and even through the night. Roger slowly rows their boat on the left side of the dirty stream of water leaving the other side free for boats going the other way. With interest Roger and Brian watch as boats similar to their own pass them heading in the direction they have come from. It is busy down here and they have boats in front of them as well as behind them also heading towards the town centre like themselves. Even the grubby but dry banks along the edges of the Rats Underground are crowded with less fortunate rats who travel simply by walking to their destination. Some of these walking rats are carrying things, some plod along with their hands tucked into their pockets daydreaming. Others walk in twos or threes chatting as they travel along and many travel alone, often hurrying.

'Busy today,' Brian observes.

'Yes, a very busy highway,' Roger agrees.

'Yeah, really gets crowded down here, some days,' adds Brian.

'I don't like it when it's like this. Bow to stern with other boats is not my idea of fun,' admits Roger.

Though he is aware of other boats full of rats all in a hurry to get somewhere, Roger just keeps rowing. He thinks about where he is going and he just hopes the traffic clears soon. His arms are beginning to get tired and traffic is made worse when someone stops rowing.

They are now further through this dark busy highway on the R.U. and it is only now that they realise why the traffic is so heavy and slow moving...

When a toilet is flushed the whole contents get carried down into the dark smelly sewers and occasionally this can cause a nasty blockage, now two rats are working hard with a pick and shovel. With great effort they are trying to clear this horrible mess which is blocking the path of all the rats who are using this busy stretch of the R.U.

As Roger and Brian know only too well clearing the R.U. is a very dirty, smelly but very necessary job, one these two friends have to do every Monday and seeing the two rats busily working in their green all in one R.U. overalls and baseball cap is a sight familiar to the two friends. The overalls are not only good at protecting the rats doing dirty work but the R.U. logo which is the yellow R above left of a yellow U in a blue circle is very good at letting travellers on the R.U. know who is mending their highways.

Eventually Roger and Brian pass the rats clearing the mess, they are soon glad to find the traffic now flowing along quite easily. Everything is quieter and their journey to Hastings House, the head office of the R.U. is now much smoother.

'Hey Rog, shouldn't we have worn our uniforms?' Brian asks, after some thought.

'What, our green overalls? And baseball cap? No, we're ok as we are,' replies Roger.

'Are you sure?'

'Well, the Herald never said, did he?'

'No, that's true, he didn't,' agrees Brian.

'Anyway, surely the Chair-rat doesn't want us standing there in our dirty smelly overalls,' adds Roger.

'No, good point. Wouldn't be nice that, yuk!' Brian realizes.

Instead Roger and Brian are heading towards Hastings House, the head office of the Rats Underground Southwest Drains Region to see the Chair-rat in their own very casual clothes. Which as usual means Roger is wearing his pale brown corduroy trousers and his baggy red sweatshirt over his pale blue T-shirt with R A T in dark blue letters on the front. Brian, as is his habit, is wearing pale blue jeans and a dark blue hooded NYR top. Being quite chilly down here on the R.U. away from the shining sun Brian has his hood up and seeing his breath decides for now that it will stay up over his head.

'Oh look Rog, it's the Farmhouse family,' calls Brian.

While still rowing Roger looks over his shoulder and sees a boat coming towards them. In the other boat are five rats, the mother, father and their three noisy, playful young little rats.

They are called the Farmhouse family because they all live in the old farmhouse not far from where Roger and Brian live. It is no longer used as a farmhouse since the town and many houses are now built around the place, but everyone knows it was once a farmhouse and the name has stuck.

'They must be on their way home from town,' suggests Roger.

'I guess so, let's ask them,' says Brian, and quickly he calls 'Hello Mrs Farmhouse, been to town?'

'Hello Brian, yes we're very busy today,' she replies.

'Yes, not stopped yet, been going for hours too!' Mr Farmhouse adds.

'Be quiet you three! Sorry about that, they're bored.'

Mrs Farmhouse apologizes for their little rats who are busy shouting and arguing among themselves, by now their boats are side by side in the R.U.

'How's the Farmhouse?' asks Roger.

'Oh it's fine thanks. You know our little place? Just beneath the front door, nice but can be busy with people coming and going.' Mr Farmhouse replies.

'You should both come round for tea one night.' Mrs Farmhouse invites.

'That'll be nice, thank you.' says Roger.

'We must go now, we're ordered to Hastings House!' Brian explains.

'Oh dear, better let you go then,' Mr Farmhouse responds.

'Bye!' they all call to each other and soon both boats are on their way in opposite directions.

'What's he mean, "Oh dear"?' asks Brian a little worried.

'Um… Well… I don't know,' answers Roger.

'Oh good, or oh really, but "Oh dear"?' thinks Brian out loud.

'Yes, a bit odd that,' admits Roger.

'You'd think he'd be pleased,' Brian replies, almost complaining.

'Yes, or amazed,' adds Roger.

Roger and Brian are not too far from Hastings House, the R.U. head office, now they turn their little rowing boat up into a very dark narrow tunnel. Only the small stub of candle glowing dimly on the bow of their boat lights their way, but it is enough.

Eventually in front of their boat they see what they have been looking for, they see the surprisingly grand entrance to the head office of the Rats Underground Southwest Drains Region.

Hastings House

In front of the two friends is a solid round door, this fits neatly into the pipe which leads into the head office, it is a fairly heavy wooden door painted a very shiny black. Above this very shiny black round door is the emblem of the Rats Underground. The yellow R and U in a blue circle is above this proud and stern looking door and no rat is going to mistake this sealed entrance for anything else. And just to make sure, to the right of the round door is a very small and grubby brass plaque. On this plaque it reads "Southwest Drains. Chair-rat Jeremy Brown".

Roger and Brian have been this way once or twice before but not often. Seeing this door they now know for certain they have arrived in the right place. Now they tie their boat up and step ashore, it only remains for them to gain entry. Strangely and worryingly the door has a guard standing right in front of the shiny black round door. The guard is a huge rat, he is so big that he would need to duck to walk through the round door. Oddly he is dressed very much like a policeman, he even wears a helmet perched firmly on his head, this helmet is not very big though, it just sits between his furry rat ears which are forced out sideways. On his helmet like everywhere else is the R.U. logo, this time it is a shiny silver colour.

Slowly but determined, Roger and Brian approach the huge guard in his policeman-like uniform, it is clear that to gain entry they will need to speak to him.

'Roger and Brian, to see the boss,' Roger announces.

'That's us,' Brian adds, pointing at himself and Roger.

Slowly and surely the guard looks Roger and Brian up and down, first one, then the other, he does not say a single word. Despite his job being simply to stand guard outside a shiny door in the gloom all day while wearing a uniform he seems to be very proud. The two friends sense they are being checked over and also sense he does not like what he sees. This does not bother them too much, they are not here to see him, they are here to see the Chair-rat, now they are beginning to wonder if the guard understands them.

'The boss, the Chair-rat,' explains Brian.

'Jeremy Brown,' adds Roger.

'Is he expecting you?' the guard finally asks.

'His Herald got us out of bed,' explains Brian.

'So I would say yes,' adds Roger.

Again Roger and Brian are forced to wait in silence as this proud guard gives them another long look up and down.

Whether he enjoys his little bit of power guarding a door below ground in the gloom or whether he needs plenty of time to think the two friends can only guess. Whatever the guard's reason for his long distrustful silences Roger and Brian are beginning to lose their patience.

'Well?' they both snap.

'Oh very well, you can come in,' the guard sighs.

Slowly and reluctantly the guard carefully opens the shiny black round door. With great interest Roger and Brian take their first look inside before entering. The door is now open enough and they step inside.

'Go straight to the desk. They will deal with you there,' explains the guard.

Before they can turn around and say anything they are almost shocked to find the door is firmly shut behind them.

'So, this is Hastings House,' says Brian, nervously.

'Yes, not easy to get in either,' notes Roger.

'Or out,' adds Brian.

For the first time in their little lives Roger and Brian get their first view of the head office of the Rats Underground in the southwest. Though many rats work for the R.U. and many more travel on the R.U. very few ever get to enter Hastings House. Despite their nervousness the two friends consider themselves privileged and even lucky to be here. A little in awe and amazement they both look around staring at their surroundings, to their surprise they find themselves in a rather large square room. Not something they would expect to find below ground among so many pipes and tunnels. The room they are standing in is more than double their own height and longer and wider still, there is a red carpet fitted wall to wall and the walls are plain concrete with patterned cloth covering them like wallpaper.

'Tapestries,' mutters Roger.

'What?' asks Brian.

'Them big pieces of cloth on the walls, I think they're called tapestries,' Roger replies.

'Oh right, I see,' says Brian, confused.

'Once upon a time-.'

'You're not going to tell me a story?' asks Brian.

'No, I was just going to say that centuries ago they used to have such things hanging in castles,' explains Roger.

'Oh ok, what no wallpaper?'

'No,' replies Roger.

The two friends have not stopped staring at this large underground room in Hastings House and the more they look the more they are impressed and even a little unnerved. Clearly this is a place run by powerful rats wishing to show off. The policeman-like guard at the door and the fancy décor to the uncomfortable silence is making Roger and Brian feel awkward in this large room. They are beginning to get the feeling that all the rats that work in here are a stern serious bunch, laughing and talking loudly the two friends suspect would be frowned upon.

At the far end of this big room, in the right hand corner is a desk. Behind this desk sit's a middle aged grey furred female rat calmly but busily dealing with paperwork. Everything about this rat is grey. Apart from her grey fur she is wearing a grey suit, jacket and skirt, she even wears a grey hairband keeping the fur on her head neat and tidy. Making Roger and Brian feel less confident this rat also wears a rather bossy look on her face, like a teacher waiting for the first sign of naughtiness and ready to punish. Cautiously the two friends approach her desk.

'Um, er... Excuse me,' asks Brian.

The grey female rat looks up, she does not smile but she is at least seems more polite than the guard.

'Yes?' she asks.

'We've come to see Jeremy Brown,' whispers Roger.

'The Chair-rat,' adds Brian, quietly.

'Yes, quite. Is he expecting you?' she asks.

Roger and Brian's nerves are now beginning to fray, they feel out of place and out of their depth. They are in a room run by important and powerful rats and the door they came in is now shut, also twice they have been asked if they are expected by rats who seem to look down at them. Roger and Brian wish they had never been ordered here.

'Yes, he summoned us here,' answers Brian.

'Good!' she replies.

Roger wonders why "good" but he is not going to ask. Get in, get out, is his plan and the sooner the better. He just hopes that they are both getting a reward or something for all their hard work, if not he dreads to think why they have been summoned.

'Sir is not quite ready to see you yet so follow me and I shall show you to the Viewing Gallery,' she announces.

This stern rat all in grey stands up and to their great surprise she smiles at them, but just as quickly as the smile appears it disappears.

'Well, follow me,' she calls.

Not wishing to get lost or be left behind the two friends hurry to keep up with her as she walks very quickly leading them to the viewing gallery.

'Viewing gallery?' asks Brian.

'Sir?' adds Roger.

Moving quickly the two friends follow the grey female rat, they do not go far but after a few turns to the left and right both feel that they might become lost if they had to retrace their steps.

'Here you are. Wait here and someone will collect you when sir is ready. Oh by the way enjoy the view!' says the grey female rat and she is gone.

Now Roger and Brian find themselves alone in what is called the Viewing Gallery, and quickly they discover why. It is cold dusty and draughty in here and they just stand on bare concrete but they are not really that bothered. Instead they stand staring at the interesting view through the holes in the air brick allowing air to circulate in the building. Also the Viewing Gallery is very close to a little shop that serves travellers arriving and leaving the busy bus station and the two friends can see people to their left reappearing with newspapers or bars of chocolate in their hands.

This vent in the wall allows Roger and Brian to take in the sights, sounds and even the smells of the bus station beyond the air brick. They hear the loud chugging of the engines as buses arrive or get ready to leave again. Occasionally they hear a bleep, bleep sound as a bus warns that it is reversing, and naturally in such a busy place they can hear the familiar noises made by people getting on with their busy lives.

Standing in a cold place with a draughty air brick as a window the two friends can even breath in the smells and fumes of the bus station. With so many diesel engines revving and ticking over, Roger and Brian inhale lots of smoky air and they find it difficult not to cough.

Many of the buses in the bays have their doors open letting passengers board when they are ready and standing where they are Roger and Brian believe they can even smell the dusty seats on the nearest two buses in front of them. Roger and Brian have hitched a ride on buses before and this smell reminds them of travel.

'I like travel Roger.'

'Me too,' Roger replies.

'That smell reminds me of holidays,' says Brian.

'Yeah, and having fun,' says Roger.

'Exploring,' adds Brian.

'Seeing new places,' agrees Roger.

Still looking at the view they both daydream, the desire to travel has returned. They look up at the buses and read the destinations beside the numbers and imagine going to these places. Right in front of them sits a long white and orange bus and it says that it is going to Oxford. To its right sits another white and orange bus and this one says Cheltenham. Further down a double-decker bus waits already half full of passengers but they cannot see what this one says.

The whole place is busy, many buses have passengers on board waiting eagerly for their driver to begin the journey. Others have long queues waiting for the driver to let them on board. Roger and Brian see this and think that people must love travel even more than them.

'Brian, look over there.'

Brian looks left in the direction his friend is pointing with his little furry paw and sees a long white coach parked in an end bay. This coach is almost full up with passengers with barely any empty seats but it is going nowhere yet. It still has doors open along its sides and several suitcases stand waiting to be put in there by the large sweating driver. Slowly the driver struggles to load the coach and one by one the remaining passengers board the coach once they know their cases are loaded.

'That coach goes to London,' explains Roger.

'What, same as the trains?' asks Brian.

'Yes. Strange really, I suppose people like to choose how to get there,' answers Roger.

Meet Jeremy Brown the Chair-Rat

They are still waiting to see the Chair-rat but are happily distracted by the views of the bus station and they are soon quiet and alone in their own thoughts. When not at home relaxing, Roger and Brian like to travel occasionally to stretch their legs and even their minds. Now they are both daydreaming about travelling, thinking about where they would like to go, how they would like to get there and what to do when they arrive. But the reason they are here in Hastings House creeps back into their minds. They have never been summoned to the head office of the Rats Underground Southwest Drains Region before and certainly not by the Chair-rat himself! Still hopefully they can be rewarded and leave quickly and return to their quiet peaceful day at home.

'Follow me,' a voice says.

Roger and Brian turn around to see who has spoken to them but the speaker is already walking away. What they see is an old, tall and rather broad-shouldered rat in grey pin-striped trousers and a long black coat, this rat is dressed much like a butler they notice. Above the collar of the black coat they can just see a whiskery grey head and ears, while between the flaps of the long black coat they see his long pink tail dragging along the ground.

'Hey Brian, we're following a well-dressed tail,' Roger whispers.

'Yeah, we are!' laughs Brian.

Away from the little bit of natural light from the air brick Hastings House is lit by little stubs of candles which give plenty of light for them to see by, though knowing their way round and not getting lost is another matter.

Suddenly the butler stops walking without any hint or warning at a round door, he knocks firmly twice and walks away. He does not say a word to Roger or Brian, he just leaves them standing at a knocked door.

'Did you get to see his face?' asks Brian.

'No, not even a glimpse,' admits Roger.

'Nor me. Weird this place,' adds Brian.

'Enter!'

From behind the closed round door a voice calls. Being the only ones waiting to enter the two friends realize they have permission to go in, but they cannot help but feel nervous. Reluctantly and nervously they open the door and enter the room.

They enter a large and mostly empty room. At the far end is a desk with a tall, thin rat in a tight grey badly-fitting suit and this rat still has his head down as he is busily writing something. Roger and Brian think the Chair-rat must be writing something important so they wait in silence and stare at the large portrait hanging on the wall behind the desk above the Chair-rat's head.

Finally after a short wait the busy Chair-rat for the Rats Underground Southwest Drains Region folds up the paper he was writing on and the two friends see the half-completed crossword puzzle.

'Sorry about that, terribly busy around here,' apologizes the Chair-rat.

For the first time Jeremy Brown, the Chair-rat looks up and sees Roger and Brian standing there in his office.

'Ah, no uniform, how… casual,' mutters the Chair-rat.

Awkwardly Roger and Brian look down at themselves seeing how they are dressed, then they look at each other. Curiously they wonder why the chair-rat would order them to the head office on their day off and expect them to appear in their dirty, smelly overalls.

'Oh well, never mind...' sighs the Chair-rat, adding 'Anyway I'm Jeremy Brown, the Chair-rat but you can call me Sir.'

'Oh, thank you,' replies Roger.

'Um, Sir,' adds Brian quietly.

'Now,' begins the Chair-rat, 'I have a quest for you.'

Not knowing what a quest is Roger and Brian just stare at him in silence, neither wish to admit to not knowing what a word means to the Chair-rat, instead they just stand looking puzzled.

'A task,' explains the Chair-rat.

Yet still they stand silently, none the wiser. It is funny how your brain does not seem to work so well when you are nervous thinks Brian to himself.

'A job,' says Jeremy Brown, the busy Chair-rat, impatiently.

'Oh, a job!' responds Roger, finally understanding.

'Oh... A job,' says Brian, unhappily.

'Yes. A job,' agrees the Chair-rat.

Now he is understood he stands up and gains their attention by pointing at the large portrait on the wall behind his desk. The painting is a full length portrait of a rat in a very old-fashioned costume. The rat in the picture is standing up with his chin held high and a paw on one hip, but most notable is his head. On his head he is wearing a great big curly white wig which reaches down to his shoulders. Brian's first impression is that he was a judge, except that the wig is too big and fancy for that. Then, there are also the clothes, instead of drab dark clothing worn by a judge this rat is wearing colourful fancy things. He is wearing a great long burgundy cloak and frilly white collar and frilly cuffs hanging over his paws, and on his legs are very tight beige leggings which only just reach the knees.

Seeing this, Roger considers how worrying fashions are; this rat was unfortunate enough to be able to afford an artist, now everyone can see how silly he looked. But now we have cameras to capture us wearing things we think look good. Still hoping he is not going to look daft in years to come Roger notices a date on the painting, it says 1803, that is really old.

'This, my very casual looking rats, is my ancestor and co-founder of the Rats Underground and his name is Nelson Brown. He, along with about two hundred others, decided to use the sewers as a home, a place to hide from danger, and above all a means of travelling in safety. So you can see how special he is and how important to the R.U.' declares Jeremy Brown, Chair-rat and relative.

'Um yeah,' agrees Roger, politely.

'Two hundred others?' observes Brian, though quietly.

'So you can see what a unique and truly special rat he was and I'm proud of him,' Jeremy Brown adds.

They do not know whether he ignored Brian's remark about the two hundred other rats involved in founding the Rats Underground or simply never heard. What they do know is that their Chair-rat is now on a roll. Clearly he is boasting about his own family and they suspect he likes the sound of his own voice.

'And this is where we get to the reason I summoned you two here today,' says Jeremy Brown.

The Chair-rat finally gets to the point. Roger and Brian have been wondering. They have not quite given up hope of being rewarded for all their hard work but even they realize that is looking doubtful. A quest, a task, a job says the Chair-rat, deep down they just know they are going to be very busy.

'We were wondering,' admits Roger.

'Sir,' adds Brian quickly.

'I am a proud rat,' Jeremy Brown, Chair-rat of the Rats Underground Southwest Drains Region announces proudly.

This the two friends realized soon after walking into his office, but wisely they stand and wait in silence. He will eventually say what he wants, that they are sure.

'And with my family's long tradition here I am proud to be the Chair-rat of the Rats Underground,' adds the Chair-rat loudly.

Still the two friends stand by his desk waiting in silence, now they wish he would get to the point.

'Which is why I wish you to get a statue to display at a busy crossroads in the R.U.,' he finally announces.

Like earlier, Roger and Brian stand staring at their Chair-rat in puzzled silence, seeing the baffled looks on their faces he realizes more information is needed.

'My ancestor was called Nelson and the statue is also of a famous Nelson.' he adds, boastfully.

'Um...?' utters Brian.

'It will look great in the R.U.,' the Chair-rat sighs.

'What does it look like?' asks Roger.

'Well erm... You see ah, well. I don't know,' the Chair-rat admits sitting back down.

'You don't know?' asks Brian.

'Well it's a column or something.'

'A column?' repeats Roger.

'Yes! That's it. Have you heard of it?' asks the Chair-rat hopefully.

'No.' the two friends answer.

'Oh... Well you have now, it's famous you know!'

'Where is this famous statue sir?' asks Brian.

'It's... On a column, I do believe. I thought I'd explained that,' the Chair-rat adds unhelpfully.

'No I meant...' tries Brian.

Jeremy Brown, Chair-rat of the Rats Underground Southwest Drains Region is a very busy rat. Deep within the head office of Hastings House he spends his day between paperwork and giving orders. After giving orders to Roger and Brian he returns to his unfinished crossword puzzle.

'Anyway never mind, I'm busy so goodbye, good luck and I'll see you both again soon, with my statue.'

Jeremy Brown leaves his desk and quickly ushers the two friends out of his office before closing the door firmly behind them.

The Quest Begins...

The two friends feel frustrated, confused and disappointed, with all this on their minds as they make themselves comfortable back in their little rowing boat.

They feel frustrated because their Chair-rat has given them a job to do and they know they must do this, somehow. They feel confused because the Chair-rat has told them very little; a statue of Nelson, somewhere on a column or something, even he does not know. The two friends also feel disappointed, they were awoken today by a Herald who sent them to the head office. They go there with a mixture of nervousness and hope as it is not everyday a rat is summoned to Hastings House and it must be really important. They manage to convince themselves they are going to be rewarded when they arrive but are given a job to do instead.

'You and your silly idea! Be rewarded!' complains Brian.

'My silly idea?' retorts Roger, hotly.

'Yes, maybe we're being rewarded for all our hard work you said.'

'Yeah, maybe I said. It's not my fault the Chair-rat's an idiot,' Roger replies with irritation.

'No, that's true,' admits Brian calmly. 'Sir?' he questions.

Roger and Brian sit facing each other in their boat in silence. They both know they have no choice but to get their Chair-rat's statue.

'What are we going to do Rog?' asks Brian.

Roger lets out a loud huff before answering his friend's question.

'I have no idea Brian. Do you know anything about this statue of Nelson?'

'No. Which makes three of us. The Chair-rat was no help, eh Rog?'

'Fancy wanting something when you know nothing about it,' remarks Roger.

Brian unties the boat and Roger begins rowing but again the two friends fall silent. They are wondering how they are going to solve their big problem, they do not even know where to start. After a long pause Roger decides to put together what little they do know.

'Right Brian, what we do know is this... Um, well, we have got to get a statue of Nelson, its famous...'

'And it's on a column or something, but where?' adds Brian.

'We don't know, so how do we find out..?' asks Roger.

Thinking about this the two friends fall silent yet again. The only sound is of the gentle rhythmic sloshing of the oars as their boat floats through the murky water in the cool, damp gloom of the R.U. In the darkness Hastings House soon disappears from view, but it is only when they turn the corner and re-enter the big sewer do their minds begin to work.

'It's quiet down here now Brian, rush hour is over.' notes Roger.

Brian, however, is not interested in how quiet and empty it is here now. Instead he is having ideas.

'Stop!' Yells Brian suddenly.

'What?' asks Roger.

'Stop the boat. Stop rowing. I've just had an idea!' announces Brian, feeling pleased with himself.

On hearing this news Roger stops rowing the boat and they float gently to a halt. It is not everyday that his friend has an idea and with such an important quest as theirs he is more than willing to listen to what Brian has to say.

'Why don't we see the Wise Rat of Wrought Iron Town?' suggests Brian.

'The Wise Rat of Wrought Iron Town? It's an idea I suppose.' admits Roger.

'Yeah, the Wise Rat knows everything.'

'Everything?' questions Roger.

'Well, lots of things,' answers Brian.

Roger and Brian turn their boat around and return to Hastings House. Once there they tie their boat up. This time they are leaving the Rats Underground and going above ground to catch a bus. It is a little bit dangerous for the two friends, they have to dodge the legs of bored and impatient people waiting to catch a bus. So they quickly seek the bus to Wrought Iron Town while trying not to be trodden on by any person. Roger and Brian hope not to be noticed because they know people do not tend to like seeing rats much but this makes it easier to get squashed by someone not seeing them. Seeing the bus they need they quickly run towards it while steering clear of the many shoes coming too close.

It is such a busy place, men, women, some noisy and playful children, and worryingly they even hear a dog bark somewhere in the distance. People here are all waiting to go somewhere, to work, home after shopping, daytrips even. Whatever the reasons, it makes Roger and Brian's plan to catch a bus difficult and dangerous. Running, the two friends only just manage to reach their bus without suffering any injury.

'Here we are!' calls Brian.

'Good. I don't know how many times my tail nearly got trodden on,' complains Roger.

'It might be quick by bus but it's not much fun getting on one, eh Rog?' notes Brian.

After so much effort and so many risks the two friends make a final leap onto the bus. Unfortunately for the two friends as they leap the bus doors shut and the bus reverses out of its bay, it is all they can do to just hold on and hitch a ride from the outside. As the bus begins its journey to Wrought Iron Town they realize this is going to be a scary trip.

'Oh well, here we go,' calls Roger.

They can already feel the wind in their faces and fearful they hold on very tight.

In a matter of minutes the bus climbs a hill lined with shops either side where it stops briefly.

'Are we there yet?' asks Brian, hopefully.

They are both feeling tired and windswept, being rats they are only little and holding on outside a moving bus is hard work. Both quietly wish they travelled on the R.U. instead, a longer but safer journey would be better than this.

'No, not yet,' answers Roger.

Once passengers have got either on or off the bus it continues its journey up the hill and the two friends hold on tight ready to feel the wind in their faces again. Round the corner it passes more shops and a few cafes where it stops once more.

'Are we there yet?' asks Brian, again.

'No, not yet,' Roger answers again.

Roger is patient with Brian, he shares his friend's eagerness to get off the bus as holding on tight is not fun. It is tiring and scary but they are getting closer to Wrought iron Town.

'Well where are we then?' asks Brian.

'This is the Old Town we're passing through,' answers Roger.

'So we're not there yet then?' questions a displeased Brian.

'No, not there. Not yet,' Roger confirms.

Now the bus leaves the Old Town and its shops behind and makes its way down a hill. This one has a wide road with nice big posh houses.

'Is this it?' yells Brian, more desperately now.

The bus does not even stop here but Brian cannot help but ask all the same. Roger wishes it was Wrought Iron Town, his arms are aching from holding on and they are almost breathless with the effort and from the wind in their faces.

'No, unfortunately it's not,' answers Roger.

'Pity, it looks nice here,' observes Brian.

It is a long road downhill but it does not stop, instead it sails past the empty bus stop and trundles along. There is no quick rest here for the two friends, they hold on as tight as ever.

Next the bus reaches a bridge. As the bus drives over the bridge Roger and Brian get a clear view below, a view they have never seen before. Below they can see the motorway with cars, vans, lorries and coaches going along fast in both directions.

'Where are they going?' mutters Roger.

Roger is thinking out loud so it surprises him when he discovers Brian can answer his question.

'London is that way and Bristol the other.'

'Oh, thanks Brian.'

'No problem,' he replies.

Quickly the bus is over the bridge and now they find themselves among more houses, a farm and then they see a hospital.

'This is Wrought Iron Town. Whereabouts does the Wise Rat live Brian?' asks Roger.

'They say he lives below the shops. There is a crossroads down there, where two main routes of the R.U. meet,' answers Brian.

'The shops, ok, we should be there in a minute,' Roger guesses.

This cheers them both up, not only can they stop holding on for fear of falling they are a step nearer solving their quest. It pleases them both when they see the shops.

'Here we are!' exclaims Brian.

Eagerly the two friends leap down from the bus the moment it stops and they are in such a hurry that the people also leaving the bus do not notice them.

'It's so good to be safely on the ground again,' admits Roger with great relief.

Now they can begin looking for the Wise Rat of Wrought Iron Town and they head quickly for the square where there is the small quiet group of shops used by the local people.

'Mmm chips...' sighs Roger.

'Yeah,' sniffs Brian. 'I'm hungry now,' he adds.

The first shop they notice is not the nearest to them, it is not the newsagent, it is not the chemist, nor is it the supermarket. With the aid of their whiskery noses and their empty stomachs the first shop they notice is the chip shop. The lovely, mouth-watering smells are almost torture especially as they know they are unlikely to have any of these hot tasty chips.

To escape the torment of smelling tasty food they cannot eat and avoid being seen by people doing their shopping Roger and Brian quickly slide down a drain and enter the Rats Underground.

Suddenly it is like being in a different world. The clean pavement and broad daylight with the nice food smells are now above and beyond them. Now it is replaced by the dark, damp gloom with its creepy echoes and the stale smell of slow flowing murky water.

The Rats Underground is not usually considered a pretty place, like all rats Roger and Brian like it simply because it serves them so well. The R.U. is a place to live and travel in safety.

The Wise Rat of Wrought Iron Town

With the gentle sounds of water gurgling and dripping Roger and Brian begin their search for the Wise Rat of Wrought Iron Town. But they soon realize they are not familiar with this part of the Rats Underground and they do not even know where to begin looking.

'Which way Rog?' asks Brian.

Roger has a good look around. He peers into the darkness one way seeing only the concrete tunnel with water at the bottom going in a straight line until the black gloom means they can see no further. He turns and looks the other way and sees much the same, only this way curves to the left. They see no crossroads.

'Um… Well, start here and go that way,' suggests Roger.

'Round the bend?'

'Yeah, might lead to the crossroads you mention,' hopes Roger.

'Yeah, we find that and we should find him,' adds Brian.

So not knowing their way the two friends begin walking along the dry bank close to the murky water towards the bend. Once round the bend they see an opening on their left.

'This way, I reckon Rog,' suggests Brian.

'Ok. Good job it's on our side or we would have to try and jump across,' observes Roger.

'Yeah and we always get something wet, a foot or our tails…' Brian admits.

They turn into the opening on their left and instantly they see a very promising view ahead. In front of them is a crossroads, a place under the ground where two sewers cross, much like two roads only more wet and dirty. This is easy for them to see because it is lit from above by a storm drain and on a large concrete plinth, like a cold hard stage sits a rat.

'Look Rog, the crossroads!' declares Brian, excitedly.

'Yeah, and look a rat over there,' Roger replies.

'I hope it's the Wise Rat,' says Brian.

'Me too, he's where the Wise Rat should be, so we should be ok,' suggests Roger, hopefully.

They reach the crossroads and climb up onto the concrete plinth but once they are there they discover the rat sitting there has gone. Roger asks the obvious question;

'Where is he? He was here a minute ago,' says Brian, looking around.

'Maybe he's popped out,' suggests Roger.

'Well I hope he's not gone long, I don't want to be here all night,' Brian says.

'Me neither, once we know where this statue is we've got to go and get it anyway,' Roger recalls.

The two friends are torn between going and searching for the Wise Rat of Wrought Iron Town or standing here waiting for him to return. Still undecided the two friends take advantage of the high position of the concrete plinth and look around the crossroads. They look everywhere in the crossroads and with the light pouring in above their heads they can see very well. They look down all four concrete tunnels with the water running slowly away hoping for a sight of the Wise Rat but the only rats here are them.

'See anything Rog?'

'No, not a thing. What about you?'

'No, nothing, not a thing. Nobody,' Brian replies.

'Can I help you?' asks a voice.

Until the sound of an unfamiliar voice Roger and Brian thought they were alone, this startles the two friends so much that they jump, they even let out a yelp of fear. Finding you are not alone can be quite unnerving and on this occasion it has shocked Roger and Brian making their little hearts race. Calming down a little bit they turn to see who has spoken to them and they see a large female rat standing beside them.

She is wearing two large fluffy pink towels, one wrapped around her body and the other wrapped like a turban around her head covering her ears. Making herself comfortable she sits down on the plinth with her legs hanging over the side.

'Who are you?' Roger and Brian ask together.

'I, am the Wise Rat of Wrought Iron Town!' she replies, proudly.

'You?' questions Roger, with surprise.

'You're a girl,' observes Brian, quickly.

'And? Are you suggesting I cannot be wise because I'm not a boy? Is wisdom strictly a male thing?' she replies.

This neither Roger or Brian have thought about, they simply assumed that the Wise Rat would be a fat old male rat. Seeing a female rat wrapped in two pink fluffy towels is not what they expected.

'Um, no, it's not,' agrees Roger.

'Sorry,' Brian apologises.

'Wasn't thinking,' admits Roger.

'No, I think. You need to if you are going to be wise,' she replies.

A silence follows briefly while Roger and Brian dwell on what the Wise Rat has just said to them. With the two friends standing there the Wise Rat is beginning to wonder what they are doing there at the crossroads in the R.U. she calls home.

'Why are you here?' she asks.

'We're looking for you,' answers Brian.

'Ah! Well, you've found me!' she observes.

'We've come to ask you some questions,' explains Roger.

'Ask away,' she invites.

The Wise Rat takes a deep breath and closes her eyes in concentration. She is now ready for their questions.

'The Chair-rat wants us to get a statue of Nelson, which is on a column or something,' Brian begins.

'But we don't know where it is or what it looks like,' Roger admits.

'And nor does the Chair-rat,' adds Brian.

This thought reminds him of their meeting with the Chair-rat. He is such an important rat and yet he remembers their meeting with some displeasure.

'So, we're hoping you can tell us something that will help us find the statue,' says Roger.

'Do you know what we are looking for or where it is?' asks Brian.

After listening to their tale the Wise Rat of Wrought Iron Town thinks deeply on their words. Now she takes a deep breath preparing to speak. In great hope Roger and Brian hold their breath and wait for the Wise Rat's answer. They do not wish to miss a single word she has to say, but the tension is unbearable.

'Can you tell us where it is then?' prompts Brian, finally.

'No,' the Wise Rat answers.

'What?' they ask together.

'No, I do not know anything about this statue of Nelson or a column,' she replies.

'Oh,' grunts Brian, disappointed.

'But I do have a suggestion for you,' she offers.

Roger and Brian's hopes quickly turned to disappointment and now they turn to hope again. They will listen to any idea the Wise rat has to offer them because they have no idea of their own.

'The way I see it you need to know what it is and where to find it,' she says.

'Yeah we've worked that bit out,' Roger says with a lack of patience.

'So go somewhere that has information,' she suggests.

'Is that it?' asks Brian frustrated.

'We knew that much, it's why we are here,' adds Roger, equally frustrated.

'Are you saying you both do not know where to get information?' she asks.

'Um... Well...' mutters Brian.

The Wise Rat lets out a long, heavy sigh, now she is feeling frustrated, this she thinks is beginning to look like a bad day.

'Well!' she says.

Like two naughty schoolchildren the two friends stand silently neither daring to speak, sensibly they wait for the Wise Rat to calm down and speak again.

'Try the library, lots of books there, you might learn something. Failing that try the Information Centre,' the Wise Rat finally answers.

'Oh yeah, thank you,' replies Roger.

'Yes, thank you,' adds Brian.

Quickly Roger and Brian turn to leave the Wise Rat in peace and to get on with whatever a Wise Rat wrapped in two pink fluffy towels does when left alone.

Just as they begin walking Brian has a thought. Before leaving he asks one more question for the Wise Rat.

'Oh by the way, what's your name?'

'Shirley,' she replies.

'Nice name,' replies Brian.

'Thank you Shirley,' adds Roger. 'Why are you here?'

'I like to watch the world go by and a crossroads is such a busy place,' Shirley explains.

Roger and Brian look around this crossroads and notice that it is dead quiet, nobody is there apart from them and there is not even any sound to be heard of rats in the R.U.

'Busy?' questions Brian.

'Yes, very,' she replies.

'Anyway goodbye! Come on Brian, time to go,' declares Roger, suddenly eager to leave.

The Sun is Shining

Once they reach the grating of the storm drain Roger and Brian haul themselves up into the peaceful square that has a few small but useful shops. Though far from crowded it still has some people quietly doing a little bit of shopping here and leaving the R.U. the two friends would normally be worried. They sense on this occasion they will be quite safe.

'The Wise Rat of Wrought Iron Town was helpful, eh Rog?' says Brian.

'Shirley? Yeah, it was worth seeing her,' agrees Roger.

Living and travelling in the sewers that make up the Rats Underground they are both very used to the damp, chilly gloom, so it is a pleasant treat for them to find the sun is shining. Instantly Brian pulls down his hood revealing the mop of black fur on the top of his otherwise white head feeling the sun's warmth. Roger takes off his baggy red sweatshirt and ties it around his waist revealing his pale blue T-shirt with R A T in dark blue letters.

'Ah, it's a nice afternoon,' Roger sighs, happily.

'The sun doesn't shine down the drains. It's nice to be up and about, eh Rog?'

Despite being sent on such a difficult quest by their Chair-rat they realise that it has made them leave their home. This has given them an opportunity to have a change of scenery and already they have met a wise and interesting rat as well as enjoying the nice weather. Now though they are thinking about catching a bus back to Hastings House where their boat is moored.

Looking and feeling totally windswept from hanging onto the outside of a moving bus the two friends leave the bright warm sunshine behind them as they re-enter the Rats Underground. Without hesitating they climb into their little rowing boat.

'Library then Rog?' asks Brian.

Unusually Roger sits back in the boat resting, his good friend Brian holds the oars ready to row the boat.

'No,' replies Roger, 'it's too late, we'll start again tomorrow.'

By the time they managed to catch a bus back to the bus station the sun was already starting to sink and riding a bus from the outside is very tiring and stressful.

'The library is probably shutting soon anyway,' agrees Brian.

'Yes. Let's go home and eat,' suggests Roger.

It has been a busy day, not the sort of day the two friends had in mind and now they are tired. They know they will not complete their quest today, they expect their quest will require a lot of time and effort. For now they would like to forget their problems. So the thought of resting and eating appeals greatly to them and Brian happily begins rowing the boat towards the storm drain near the football ground which they call home.

Friday – Library and beyond?

The library is a big red building with many tall windows letting in plenty of natural light so people can easily read their books. This is a fairly tall building with three or four floors. On top of the roof along the edge are several large round shiny metal chimneys, only these have many holes in them and they look something like giant cheese graters.

Arriving on the Rats Underground Roger and Brian carefully climb out of the storm drain which is helpfully sign-posted as "Library" by the R.U. As soon as they reach the street level they simply stand staring up at this building which is about thirty metres in front of them.

'You'd think there would be an entrance closer than this eh Rog?' Brian complains.

'You would. All these people walking around make me nervous,' admits Roger.

The library is a new building which has been built onto the town hall but being red brick it looks much the same and blends in looking just as old. Though Roger likes to read a newspaper, the R.U. News occasionally, neither of them bothers with books much and they do not come to this end of town often.

'I didn't know this library was here,' admits Roger.

'No, nor me,' Brian also admits.

'Useful to know, I suppose,' suggests Roger.

Not wishing to stand above ground all day least of all with people everywhere doing their shopping the two friends start walking towards the big new red brick library. On reaching the door they just stand there not moving, each seems to be waiting for the other to enter first.

'Shall we go in?' asks Roger.

'Might as well,' answers Brian.

It is such a new building that if there is a way in on the Rats Underground it has not been found yet. Instead Roger and Brian enter the library the same way people enter the library; through the door.

Roger and Brian nervously step through the doors and for the first time ever they see inside the new library. It is their first time in any library, living and travelling on the Rats Underground, somewhere also known as sewers they have very little need for books.

So walking into this bright clean new library is a novelty to them. Filled with curiosity they begin to look around, partly in awe at such an unexpected sight and partly wondering where to start looking for information on a statue of Nelson which is on a column.

Their bare feet enjoy walking on the soft warm fitted carpet that so far appears to cover the whole floor. Hearing a noise they look to their right and see the reception desk with a smartly dressed grey haired woman busily working. There are other people in here, mostly with their noses buried in books but seeing this woman worries the two friends and they quickly run past deeper into the library.

This is an amazing sight they think, there are many rows of bookshelves all stacked high full with many books. Towards the centre is a large table with chairs for people to sit and study, at the moment there are two people sitting at the table so Roger and Brian are extra careful not to be noticed.

'Probably too busy reading to notice us,' suggests Roger, hopefully.

'True. Best to be careful though,' advises Brian wisely.

Still looking around the library they now discover some armchairs in a quiet shady corner where people, if they wish can read in comfort. Looking the other way they see a wide sweeping staircase leading upstairs to more books, there is even a lift for those not wishing to use the stairs.

'Where shall we look Rog? Down here I hope!' asks Brian.

'Um... Well, it's a statue we're after so I reckon it must be art,' Roger guesses.

'Ok, books on art then,' agrees Brian.

Now the two friends head for the section in the library marked art, fortunately from where they are standing this section is easy to see.

Libraries are such quiet places, everyone read their books in silence and those asking questions do so in hushed tones. A library is not a place for laughing out loud or shouting and screaming. Roger and Brian have heard about this so move silently and even feel safe in such a quiet place.

Together Roger and Brian manage to pull a book about statues off the bottom shelf and open it up on the floor. Inside are pictures of many different statues but these are wobbly shaped things and they cannot make out what these statues are meant to be, whether people, animals or something else they cannot tell.

'This won't do,' mutters Roger.

The book is large and it is heavy and awkward for two little rats so they do not bother to even attempt to put it back on the shelf, instead they just leave it on the floor. Now they begin searching on the bookshelf for another book on statues, they are hoping for better luck. But their luck does change...

'Mice!' a voice screams.

This startles everyone in the library who stop reading or searching for a book and look round towards the screaming voice. Even Roger and Brian stop what they are doing after hearing the word "mice" screamed loudly.

'Where?' asks Roger.

'I think they mean us,' answers Brian.

In a normally quiet and peaceful library chaos suddenly breaks out which causes poor Roger and Brian to panic. Forgetting the book on the floor or their search for another on statues the two friends run like their little lives depend on it, but in their panic neither know which way to turn. They run in all directions, back and forth, round and round...

The once quiet readers in their panic add to the chaos, not knowing whether to catch the rodents or run away from them they manage to upturn chairs, drop books, worse still someone trips over a book left on the floor. This leads to a bookshelf being grabbed by the person trying not to fall over, unfortunately the bookshelf topples over. Crash! And books come tumbling out all over the floor making a terrible mess.

This distracts the people in the library and Roger and Brian have a moment to think, long enough for them to remember where the door is. Seeing daylight they aim for the door and safety and quickly make their escape.

After such an horrible experience the two friends head quickly and quietly for the storm drain and the safety of the Rats Underground where they stand gasping for breath.

'That was close!' pants Brian.

'Yeah... And we still know nothing about this statue of Nelson.' adds Roger, between breaths.

'I'm not going back in there!' responds Brian, quickly.

'Don't worry, neither am I,' Roger assures.

The two friends lean against the wall near the entrance of the R.U. Occasionally they stare up through the grating of the storm drain and sometimes see the legs of people walking past. This reminds them of how busy it is around here and it also makes them dwell on their lucky escape from the library.

'Information Centre next then Rog?' asks Brian.

'Yeah. I think we'll get as close as possible on the R.U. Lets go back to our boat,' Roger suggests.

'Ah, nice and safe on the R.U. Pity we can't stay on the R.U.,' Brian complains.

The quest for the column has already proven a tough and even risky business for the two friends. So far they have risked being trodden on at the bus station and been windswept holding onto the outside of a moving bus. Now they are still feeling shaken from being chased out of a library, they cannot bear to think what might have happened had they been caught. All this they have endured and they still know nothing about the statue of Nelson or the column. It is proving to be a difficult and dangerous quest.

'Oh well, let's go,' says Roger.

The two friends make their way down the Rats Underground where they climb into their boat. It is busy, this part of the R.U. and they pass many other rats travelling somewhere, it might be damp and dark but it is safe, so rats avoid the surface, much like Roger and Brian are doing.

It is not far from the library to the Information Centre and Brian, who rows this time does not need to row for long before reaching their destination. They tie their boat up and head towards the exit sign saying "Old Cinema". Walking along in the R.U. Brian suddenly stops as he notices another tunnel.

'Hey Rog! Where does that lead?' asks Brian.

Roger stops beside Brian and looks down into that long, dark and seemingly unused tunnel, there is not even an R.U. sign saying where it leads to or from.

Roger is as fascinated as Brian about this empty tunnel and any other time they would go down there just to satisfy their curiosity. But until they have finished their quest of finding the statue of Nelson for the Chair-rat they will have to put it off for another time.

'I don't know Brian, I wonder where it leads myself,' answers Roger.

Thinking of the quest Roger quickly starts walking again towards the exit on their way to the Information Centre. Not wishing to be left behind Brian quickly follows him. The problem Brian has with following his good friend Roger is simply that an Information Centre is a place used by people. This Brian knows could prove to be very useful but it means going above ground in broad daylight in the town centre on a Friday. This means a lot of people for them to try and avoid and they have already had a scary escape from the library. But they are friends and they both share the same unwanted quest of finding a statue for their Chair-rat, Jeremy Brown to display somewhere on the Rats Underground. So nervously with his friend, Brian joins Roger and heads towards the storm drain saying "Old Cinema" on a sign.

They carefully climb up through the grating and find themselves facing two pubs with some people sitting outside and the Information Centre almost next door.

'How are we going to learn anything?' asks Roger, after a long thought.

'What do you mean?' questions Brian.

'Well, we can't just walk in and ask questions,' observes Roger.

'Oh yeah, I hadn't thought of that,' admits Brian.

Neither are willing to break cover and leave the safety of the storm drain, instead they rest there pondering their problem and plucking up the courage to run above ground into the

Information Centre. Seeing all those legs of people walking around, some drifting from one shop to another and others rushing along does not help the two friends feel any better. The fear of being trodden on is added to the nasty shock of being chased out of the library, a risk they will take of happening in the Information Centre, but they have to get there first.

'We'll just have to see what we can do,' sighs Roger, after some thought.

'Oh well... Ready?' asks Brian.

'As I'll ever be. Good luck.'

'Run!' yells Brian.

Leaflets and Mice

It is only a short distance but Roger and Brian are little compared to the people towering above them, they also have to zigzag to avoid being squashed by unseeing feet. The shadows of shoes above them make Roger and Brian run faster. Fortunately they are not exposed to the danger of being trampled for long but when feeling nervous, moments like this seem to last for ages. They reach the doorway, slip into the shop and quickly hide behind a rack where they regain their breath and try to calm their frayed nerves.

From their safe hiding place the two friends take the opportunity to look around the Information Centre without being seen. To save themselves time and a lot of hassle they try and work out the layout of the place also looking for possible escape routes. But what they need most is to discover where any information on the statue of Nelson or its column can be found, if they can see this from here they can run and grab it and return to their hiding place.

'Can you see anything Brian?'

'Um… Half price tickets to an amusement park, that sounds good.' answers Brian.

'No Brian.'

'A day at the seaside, that would be nice.'

'No Brian,' repeats Roger.

'Hey look!' says Brian, excitedly.

'What?' asks Roger, hopefully.

'Canterbury cathedral, I've always wanted to go there,' replies Brian, unhelpfully.

'No Brian, I mean do you see anything about this Nelson statue, a column or... Anything?' explains Roger.

'Oh yeah, I see... No. Do you?' asks Brian.

Without leaving their hiding place behind a rack full of leaflets Roger pokes his head further round looking at the posters on the wall, lowering his eyes he sees racks full of leaflets. There are many to choose from and in such a small shop there are a few people nosing around either flicking through leaflets or asking questions at the counter. Here a woman is answering a young man's questions while they peer down studying a map. Roger returns his gaze to the leaflets and spots something of interest.

'Ah!' he exclaims.

'What?' asks Brian, keenly.

'Look there,' he points. 'Visit Scotland. I'd love to do that some day,' Roger replies.

'Visit Scotland? Still no statue of Nelson?' groans Brian.

'No. We'll have to take a better look in here,' suggests Roger, with great reluctance.

'Oh well,' sighs Brian, nervously.

'Good luck and be careful,' says Roger.

'Or quick,' adds Brian.

The two friends know that when you happen to be a rat the best thing for getting you out of trouble is speed and the next best thing is an escape route. These two things are as much on their minds as the statue of Nelson.

Quietly and very carefully they step out from their safe hideout behind the leaflet rack and begin their search for any information about statues of Nelson. Now in the open on the floor of the shop they can see so much more and many more leaflets appear in their view. They are almost distracted by the sight of many colourful leaflets, especially the ones in the rack they were hiding behind and stand staring up at them. Such a choice to look at; Places to see, things to do, some local and others far away in other parts of the country. Roger and Brian are drawn in by the sight of all these leaflets and find themselves dreaming of visiting some of these interesting places and doing some fun things. But so far they have not yet seen any sign or clue about statues of Nelson or columns or anything that might even help.

'It's no use,' complains Brian.

'Keep looking though Brian. There must be something,' hopes Roger.

The two friends are becoming disheartened but keep moving quietly while still looking for anything that might mention a statue of Nelson, something anywhere in here would be good.

After their last rather horrible experience in the library Roger and Brian are fearfully desperate not to be seen. Even though they are indoors Brian has his hood up, he has pulled it so far up over his head that it almost covers his eyes. This might make Brian feel a little bit invisible but it also ruins his ability to see where he is going, but still he keeps it hanging over his eyes.

'Brian look where you are...'

Bang! Clumsily Brian walks into a pile of leaflets stacked on the floor causing them to slide messily all over the floor.

'Going,' Roger finishes his words.

Not for the first time today Roger and Brian find themselves at the centre of chaos. A young woman seeing the leaflets suddenly sliding over the floor looks down to see Brian staggering around.

'Ah! Mice!' she yells in horror.

'Rats! We're rats!'

Brian yells at the young woman but it is no use, all she hears are the squeaks of an enraged rodent. But there is no time to stand and argue, on hearing the alarm the man who was studying a map at the counter starts yelling and thrashing around. He chases poor Roger and Brian around the shop, from somewhere a broom appears and with this the man arms himself. Roger and Brian are really scared now. Trying to escape being either caught or hurt they run wildly around the shop, squeaks from them and screams from the people. Terrified they somehow find themselves by the counter, the next moment they become split up. Despite their desperate efforts they do not reach the door, instead they run fearfully from one leaflet rack to another narrowly missing being hit by a falling pile of leaflets. Thankfully the two friends manage to meet up again but they are still terrified and chaos still surrounds them. With the shouts and screams and their own frightened squeaks they run around still being chased. They are enduring many very scary moments and both just miss being swiped by the broom, but now their luck changes; Roger and Brian suddenly realize they are by the open door.

Without hesitating the two friends leap through the door and run to freedom and safety but they are so frightened once through the door that they just keep running. They do not even consider which way they are running, at the moment the further away the better is their strong feeling. But in their haste instead of sensibly running towards the storm drain or any storm drain which would lead them to the Rats Underground they go in another direction. They realize their mistake when it is too late and not wishing to expose themselves to more danger in the street they quickly dive into a pub. Beginning to feel tired, Roger and Brian quickly find somewhere to hide beneath the fairly busy bar.

Inside the pub Roger and Brian suddenly feel as though they have entered a different world. It is not like the safe but damp and gloomy R.U. and it is not anything like the bright light of day outside where dodging people's feet is a major problem for them. Instead it is a place busy with people but they are all too busy chatting to take even the slightest notice of two scared rats seeking a quiet place to hide.

Inside the pub is dimly lit and the floor is mostly covered in a reddish carpet with a dark wooden floor around the bar, all the tables, chairs and stools are also made of dark wood. The bar where drinks are sold is also made of dark wood and some men are standing or sitting here talking and drinking, the two friends soon realize this is not a bad place to hide. In the bar at the floor is a tiny triangular gap, just big enough for them to pass through.

'Quick, in here Rog.' says Brian.

His squeaks are lost among the loud laughter and voices of the people in the pub but Roger hears him well enough and quickly follows his friend through the gap leading them into safety. Being a little bit fat Roger has a tighter squeeze than the very slim Brian who darts through but Roger is soon on the other side of the bar.

Once inside the bar the two friends sit down and have a well needed rest, they even manage to relax a little and this gives them the time to take note of where they are now. Still sitting down they look around and see clean and empty upturned pint glasses and an open box of crisps, they soon realize they are sitting on a shelf beneath the bar. Also they notice some clear plastic tubes beside them, these are like hoses and occasionally these fill up with beer which is pumped up through to the bar when a drink is being served. Sensing the people here are happily distracted and feeling a bit tired Roger and Brian decide to rest and listen to the men at the bar talking.

They are aware of two men standing at the bar as they had to sneak past them to get where they are now sitting resting. One man leaning on the bar is wearing a heavy black coat over his grubby blue overalls and though they are baggy they do not hide his large belly which sticks out a fair bit. His younger friend, however, is quite thin. He is standing up holding a half full pint glass of beer and wearing blue jeans, blue sweatshirt and white baseball cap. He talks occasionally but is mostly listening to his older friend talking about his daytrip to London.

'Yeah, tomorrow morning we shall be on the train to Paddington station,' the black coat says.

'You like London, eh John?' observes the baseball cap.

'I do! Last time we were there we went to see Nelson's Column,' adds John, the wearer of the black coat.

Roger and Brian hear his words clearly and sit up so sharply they almost kick a glass over. Now at last they have learned something about this statue.

'That's it! It's called Nelson's Column!' declares Brian.

'And it's in London,' says Roger, excitedly adding, 'lets hope they say more about it.'

Roger and Brian listen even more closely to the two men talking through the hole in the bar, they hope to learn some more. They have discovered the statue is called Nelson's Column which explains why the Chair-rat said a statue of Nelson on a column or something. Importantly they have just learned that it is in London but whereabouts and what it looks like they still do not know.

'Yeah, Nelson's Column was good... We're going to see the Houses of Parliament tomorrow! Anyway how's your dog doing Dave, he ok?' asks John, changing the subject.

'Dog? Yuk!' Brian responds.

'Come on, let's go,' says Roger.

How Dave's dog is they shall never know, not that they care to know. Instead Roger quickly stands up and dusts down his brown corduroy trousers and his baggy red sweatshirt with his paws. Brian stands up and pulls his hood down and has a good long stretch, even allowing himself a satisfying groan and then they are ready to leave.

'Go? Which way?' Brian yawns.

'This way,' answers Roger.

The Cellar

Grabbing hold of one of the plastic beer hoses that lead up from the cellar, Roger carefully slides downwards, Brian copies by grabbing hold of another beer hose and follows his friend to the cellar. The sights and sounds of the busy pub disappear as they plummet downwards and still sliding, the two friends each land neatly onto a metal barrel connected to the pipes in the cellar. They both look at each other after touching down and though landing on metal barrels, being small their feet barely make a sound. Normally a cellar is pitch dark but someone has left the light on; it is only a weak bulb giving off a dim yellowish glow but it is enough to see. Roger and Brian are glad they made little noise landing because their first thought was that someone was still in here but now know the light has been left on by mistake. Taking advantage of the light they quickly begin looking around for a way out.

'My dad used to say, "a good pub has a way in and a way out of the cellar onto the R.U." I always remember that,' explains Roger.

'Well I hope this is a good pub,' Brian remarks.

'Oh it is, I'm sure of that,' replies Roger, confidently.

The two friends climb down off the metal barrels and step onto the dry cobble stone floor of the cellar, around them there are many metal barrels lined against a brick wall. In the dim yellowish light they see a flight of wooden steps which they guess lead up to the bar and looking the other way they see a wooden hatch which is in the ceiling of the cellar. This opens up into the street above.

'That's where the barrels come through, when they're delivered,' explains Roger.

'Oh right. Did your dad tell you that?' asks Brian.

'Yeah, he used to live in pub cellars,' replies Roger.

Roger is looking towards the cellar hatch and wondering whether this will be a useful way of getting out until he sees what he is looking for, the reason they descended into the cellar. Between two barrels laying down on the cobblestone floor Roger notices a small hole in the wall.

'Ah! Here we are, the way out. Come on Brian, to the R.U!' declares Roger.

Brian is feeling relieved, they have finally learned something about their quest and now they have found their way out of the cellar. Playfully he hits one of the two barrels beside their exit and hears a hollow clang and realizes that it must be empty, he hits the other one and hears the same hollow clang.

'These must be empties ready to go,' observes Brian.

'What?' asks Roger, disinterested.

'Nothing,' mutters Brian.

The two friends walk in silence, only the sound of their bare feet gently slapping the concrete of the tunnel they are now in can just be heard. It is pitch dark even Roger and Brian cannot see and the tunnel is gently winding, all they can do is put their hands out and follow the tunnel to where ever it leads. It is such a small tunnel they can touch the sides with their outstretched hands which helps.

'Where does this lead Rog?' asks Brian, from behind.

'To the R.U.," answers Roger.

'Whereabouts?' asks Brian.

'I don't know, but once there we'll find our way,' replies Roger, honestly.

In pitch darkness the two friends keep walking along in the small tunnel, unable to see Brian begins to think about what they have discovered about their quest so far.

'I suppose we'll have to go to London now we know Nelson's Column is there,' suggests Brian.

'Yeah. And by train, seeing as it is so far,' Roger remarks, adding, 'we could easily be there by this evening.'

'What?' exclaims Brian, 'Go today? We haven't even got back to the R.U. yet.'

No sooner than Brian has finished saying these words they see a faint hint of light in front of them. After spending time in a cramped tunnel in darkness they are both eager to be free and hurry towards the light, the two friends are both delighted and surprised when they see their boat in front of them. They turn around and see the Rats Underground sign saying "Old Cinema" and next they see the old unused dark tunnel that interested them earlier.

'Hey Rog, that dark tunnel leads to the pub and we just used it.'

'Oh yeah, now we know. Must remember that, could be useful.' notes Roger. Roger is glad to be out of that pitch-dark tunnel, even though it lead them safely and quite easily back. Now they are back both climb wearily into their boat.

It has been a tiring and very frightful day so far already and yet there is still so much left to do as there is now a quest leading them to London.

'Roger, if we're going to London then we'd best go home first and get a few things,' suggests Brian wisely.

'Very true Brian. We need to be prepared and I'm hungry anyway,' admits Roger.

By the time Roger and Brian tie their boat up at the entrance of the pipe leading up to their storm drain home they are both feeling tired and a little bit sleepy as well. They walk slowly and silently up the pipe and enter their damp, draughty but otherwise cosy home and both see their own beds looking so inviting. After such a stressful start to the day and feeling quite tired the two friends decide it would do no harm to lie down for a few minutes. Roger slumps down on his bed and Brian sprawls lazily over his and after staring up at the concrete that they call their ceiling for a few moments it is not long before they both decide to rest their eyes by closing them.

Ideally a bed for Roger and Brian like any rodent would be woodchips with shredded paper on top but in a damp drain this is not practical. Instead their beds are old plastic take away food containers and for warmth each has a couple of old handkerchiefs which serve well as sheets. It is on these rather comfortable beds the two friends lie down to rest, silently they listen to the water running in the sewers below and to the sounds of birds singing in the trees above.

Roger and Brian have already had such an eventful day what with being chased out of the library then out of the Information Centre, ending up hiding in the pub where of all places they learn something. In the pub the two friends discover the statue of Nelson is in London somewhere and realize they will have to catch a train but a nice rest is needed first. After such a busy time and with such thoughts on their minds it is not very long before the two friends fall asleep.

A couple of hours have passed since Roger and Brian decided to have a quick lie down. What began as a little rest became a light doze and soon ended up as a nice long refreshing sleep. Now two hours or so have since passed and the two friends are still slowly trying to shake off their sleepiness.

'I fell asleep, Rog.'

'Me too,' Roger yawns in reply.

He sits up quickly but suddenly feels dizzy and light headed, though still feeling very groggy from sleep Roger feels a need to hurry. If they are to catch a train to London then they need to get a move on. Sleeping, Roger realizes has delayed them, he accepts though that they both must have been very tired to fall asleep so easily.

'We need to get ready Brian,' yawns Roger.

'I know but I can't quite get my head up yet,' replies Brian, also yawning.

After much grunting and groaning the two friends are almost off their warm beds... Almost.

'Can't we just go tomorrow?' suggests Brian.

'The sooner we get there the sooner we get back,' Roger answers.

'Yeah but...'

'Get the Chair-rat his statue and we are done. Best get going Brian.'

Roger does not really wish to go, he would rather just stay in bed and sleep but he is eager to get the job done so they can return to their easy life with their simple routines. Brian understands this and feels much the same way and doing this job for their Chair-rat is something they must do and the quicker the better.

Much of the groaning, yawning and complaining is over now as the two friends potter around gathering together anything they might need while away from home. Fortunately this is not much and both manage to stuff all their pockets quite full before walking down the pipe back onto the Rats Underground where their boat is tied up.

'To your mum's first Rog, you can row,' says Brian.

He hops quickly into their boat and sits down on the passenger seat leaving the other seat free for Roger.

'Thanks,' says Roger, not feeling at all grateful.

This is only a small step, just the beginning but their journey to London begins with the stroke of an oar in the murky water of the R.U. Still feeling sleepy Roger rows to his mum's home.

Roger's mum lives under the concrete floor of the signal box at the train station so it will be ideal to meet her before they catch their train. This is very useful for the two friends because Roger's mum often has a good idea of train times and where they are going.

Roger and Brian arrive at the train station on the R.U where they tie their boat up securely. They leave the R.U. by climbing up through a storm drain and begin walking towards the entrance of the train station. This they know is also used by the many people wishing to catch a train so they have the problem of not being seen while not being trodden on accidentally. The two friends enter the train station through the sliding doors and walk along a short well-lit subway lined each side with adverts for train journeys. Now the two friends feel the excitement they always feel when they begin a journey or holiday.

'I'm waking up now,' yawns Brian.

'Me too,' answers Roger.

'Hey Rog, I've just remembered, we've been to London before,' recalls Brian.

'Oh yeah, ages ago though,' replies Roger.

'We went on a passenger train with people. How we getting there this time?' asks Brian.

'I don't know, I'll ask my mum, she knows the trains here so well,' Roger replies.

The two friends walk along the subway to the end and climb up the steps and once at the top they quickly head towards platform one. Because it is so crowded by the newsagents with people simply waiting, reading or drinking coffee they do not hang around. Even once they step onto the platform the two friends keep moving because there are people here looking for the first sight of their train to appear. In daylight with little else to occupy their minds Roger and Brian know these passengers could easily spot them and they do not want to be chased for a third time today.

'It's busy here, eh Rog?' Brian observes.

He slows down to look at the people on the platform, they all seem too busy and impatient to notice anything which is not what they would expect. Roger looks around and realizes they have little chance of being noticed, which is strange he thinks.

'Of course! I've got it Brian, it's a Friday, everyone here is in a hurry to get home for the weekend,' Roger suddenly remembers. Walking down the platform they reach the end which helpfully slopes downwards where they can walk along the rail tracks, the two friends feel safe and relax here because it is too dangerous for people. Here it is still dangerous though because they are close to where the trains travel so being little they stay as far away from the tracks as possible.

'I can see your mum's home from here Rog, or the signal box that sits over it,' observes Brian.

'Yes Brian, you say that every time we come here.'

'Do I?'

'Yes.'

'Oh well, it will be a surprise for her to see us today,' suggests Brian.

'Yeah, she normally only sees us on Sundays,' agrees Roger.

The two friends walk along stepping on the gravel where wildflowers are growing. They are almost eye-level to the shiny metal rail tracks which are slightly raised. It amazes them both that such delicate flowers can grow so close to where huge fast-moving trains race past.

'Pretty here,' says Roger.

'It is, scary though when one of them trains pass,' says Brian.

'True, it's enough to take us off our feet,' notes Roger.

'I never feel comfortable when a train is in sight,' admits Brian.

He looks nervously over his shoulder half expecting a train to be almost on top of them.

'No me neither Brian, fun to watch from behind the fence though.'

When at the train station the two friends always feel safe when they are with Roger's mum, she knows this place well and also knows how to remain safe. Once they are with her in her home they begin enjoying the sights and sounds of the train station.

The Journey

Standing at the entrance beneath the signal box is a smiling friendly brown rat in a blue dress, a white apron and a red headscarf. This is Roger's mum standing in the doorway of her home.

'Hello mum,' calls Roger.

'Hello Roger's mum,' calls Brian.

'Hello you two,' replies Roger's mum.

In her spare time Roger's mum likes to watch the trains passing so close to her doorstep beneath the signal box, even if she is not watching she can hear or even feel these huge fast-moving trains thundering past. She spends a lot of her time on or around the railway tracks which is why she has such a good idea of the train times.

Being only a Friday Roger's mum does not expect to see Roger or his friend Brian.

'What are you doing here? It's not Sunday,' says Roger's mum.

'We've come to catch a train,' Roger replies.

'To London,' adds Brian.

'To London eh? Come in for a cup of tea, you've got time.'

They follow Roger's mum into her dimly lit but otherwise comfortable home. Once inside the two friends eagerly throw themselves down onto a fresh pile of woodchips in one corner and make themselves cosy. This is a luxury for them, living in a sewer woodchips would be wet and horrible but here they are dry and clean.

While they are busy lounging Roger's mum makes them all cups of tea. When they have all settled down they happily drink their tea, then Roger and Brian begin telling Roger's mum about the quest and their reason for going to London.

'So the Chair-rat wants a statue of Nelson,' says Roger.

'And there's a statue called Nelson's Column in London somewhere,' adds Brian.

'And you've been in the Chair-rat's office? The Chair-rat of the Rats Underground South-west Drains Region?' asks Roger's mum, amazed.

'Yeah,' Roger replies.

'And he's got us running around for him,' adds Brian, with frustration.

'What's it like?' asks Roger's mum.

'Eh?' Brian responds, puzzled.

'The Chair-rat's office. What's it like?' she repeats.

'Oh, it's ok, red carpet and a desk with a large picture of a strangely dressed rat behind it where he sits,' explains Brian.

'Yeah, a picture of Nelson Brown, his ancestor and co-founder of the Rats Underground,' adds Roger.

'I see, so that's the reason the Chair-rat has got you two searching for him,' Roger's mum ends.

Roger and Brian slowly finish drinking their cups of tea with Roger's mum, but it is now beginning to get late and the train which will take them to London through the night will be arriving shortly.

Fortunately living by the railway station Roger's mum knows so much that might prove useful and train times and destinations are very useful things to know. She also knows about the freight trains that pass her home beneath the signal box, the rats travelling on them tell her so much, like where they are going and even what the train is carrying.

After stepping outside Roger and Brian slowly follow Roger's mum as she calmly leads them alongside the tracks, they are making their way to where freight trains often stop. Hearing a metallic creaking and groaning sound they look over their shoulders towards the train station and its platforms and see a slow-moving train approaching.

'Is that it?' asks Brian.

'Yes, that's it,' replies Roger's mum.

The freight train rarely stops beside the platforms so the two friends with Roger's mum leads them further down the line. Now they are waiting for this great long slow-moving train to arrive at the spot where they are now waiting. Roger's mum is confident that it will grind to a halt here.

The big yellow engine pulling the great long train of many different carriages trundles slowly past them. The engine hisses and the freight carriages gently creak and groan as they pass where they stand patiently waiting for it to finally grind to a halt. With a growing sense of excitement they watch the various types of carriages carrying different kinds of freight. They see long shiny cylinders and big open skips full of gravel piled high and they see many metal boxes, also they see some wooden flatbed carriages which are empty. All these are on big solid metal wheels and being pulled by the yellow engine at the front, but the ones that interest them are the wooden boxes with the sliding wooden doors. In one of these Roger and Brian can travel easily to London.

'These are often used to take farm animals somewhere,' Roger's mum explains.

'Will there be cows or sheep inside?' asks Brian.

'Or pigs?' asks Roger.

'No, they're probably empty,' Roger's mum replies.

As is very often the case when waiting to board a train what begins as a peaceful and even lonely wait ends up a crowded and hurried affair. Roger and Brian suddenly realize they are not the only ones waiting to board the train. Standing around them are about ten other rats each impatiently waiting for the freight train to stop so they can eagerly climb aboard. Some of these rats are travelling alone while some are in small groups chatting excitedly.

With a long strangled groan and a shudder the freight train finally grinds to a complete halt.

Almost as a team a small group of impatient rats pull the sliding wooden door open making enough room so all the rats can board easily, then they quickly sit down in a dark corner together. It is now time for Roger and Brian to say their goodbyes to Roger's mum, she has been kind and helpful.

'Thank you!'

'Bye!'

'See you soon.'

And;

'Have a good journey.'

These last words being said by Roger's mum.

Now the two friends climb up into the wooden carriage and make themselves comfortable. They want to be ready for the long overnight journey ahead.

'Ah, a sleeping compartment,' sighs Roger, happily.

Because they will be travelling through the night he knows they will need to sleep and it is important to be comfortable so they do not wake up tired or achy.

Meanwhile the small group of rats, all young males, have already settled into playing dominoes and seem as though they will be cheerfully playing all night long. The lone travelling rats have settled down quite well, and though sitting separately they have already begun talking to each other. It is a long journey ahead and a bit too lonely for them if they do not speak once in a while and rats are sociable friendly creatures. This just leaves the mother with her young daughter and her very young son, these three Roger and Brian did not notice until after they had climbed aboard the train. Quickly Brian leaps down and passes the young daughter up to Roger followed quickly by the very young son and then between them they help the mother to climb up into the train.

'Thank you,' she says.

'That's ok,' replies Brian.

'Say thank you little ones,' the mother says to her children.

'Thank you misters,' they say politely.

All the rats have now settled down as comfortably as it is possible to do on the hard wooden floor of a box train and they are ready for the journey to begin, but they have to wait...

There is a long wait, a very long wait as the train sits unmoving on the tracks. Even the rats on board who travel often enough to know that these trains sometimes take ages to get moving again are beginning to wonder how much longer before it starts moving again. And even though the happily occupied, domino players who have their game to distract them they too are starting to feel impatient.

'Come on,' moans one of the lone rats.

'Get moving,' groans another.

'They're taking their time tonight,' notes a domino player with his red hood almost hiding his face.

'The driver's having a cup of tea I expect,' his friend all in black suggests.

'Good idea!' another player in a baggy brown raincoat responds.

To the surprise of every other rat in the wooden boxcar the domino players briefly stop their game and make cups of tea, enough tea is brewed for every rat on board, including the two young little rats with their mother.

Just as the tea is brewing the train shunts forward slightly and then slowly, almost cautiously begins rolling forwards. At last the night journey on the freight train to London has begun.

'Hooray!' the mother's little rats cheer.

'Tea up everyone,' announces the rat in the brown raincoat

'Bye mum,' calls Roger.

'Bye Roger's mum,' calls Brian.

Roger's mum went home for a while but returned when she saw the driver climb into the yellow engine at the front, she, too, knows they can wait around for a long time. But now they wave goodbye as the freight train, creaking and groaning takes the strain and gently picks up some speed.

Now the train is leaving the station behind Roger and Brian realize how late it is getting by the darkening sky, it is now a deep blue and a gloom is settling within their carriage. The boxcar is lit by a small stub of candle used by the domino players but it is still dark.

Grunting and groaning, clanking and creaking the long freight train soon passes a high embankment which gives all those on board a good view of the town.

But now everything is in total darkness lit only by the streetlights and the neon signs which help keep a town buzzing after dark.

Now the train begins to gather pace, it will soon reach its top speed but this is still quite slow especially compared to a passenger train which suddenly hurtles past at great speed. This causes the rats closest to the door which is still open ajar to jump with fright, even the domino players in the far corner stop and look up as the passenger train screams past. The rush of wind and flashes of light from the windows grabs everyone's attention for a few moments making their hearts race until it has past.

When this train has gone Roger and Brian discover their own train has not yet gone far and they are now only just crossing a bridge. Looking down from here they see the Kestrel Fish bar which clearly is a popular place as many people are queuing outside the door while out the other people are emerging with hot white parcels of fish and chips tucked safely under their arms. Next the train goes over a much larger bridge and looking down from this one they see a white van going over a roundabout, this the two friends know will take it past the football ground which is close to their own home. This is one thing the two friends enjoy about travelling, the opportunity to watch others getting on with their lives while they sit back, relax and simply observe. For some reason this makes Brian think of something that has nothing to do with what he can see from the open door of the train.

'Hey Rog,' he begins.

'Yes?'

'Was your mum ever a nurse?' he asks.

'Um...I don't know. Why?'

'I don't know,' admits Brian. It is a while longer before Brian has thought long enough to ask another question of his friend, the gentle rattle of the train has helped Brian order his thoughts. He is still pondering Roger's mum in her blue dress, white apron and her red headscarf, to him it is like a nurse uniform.

'Why does your mum dress like a nurse?' he pursues.

'Does she?' Roger responds, feeling puzzled.

It is a matter of only a few minutes and the slow moving freight train, gently creaking and clanking along the rails reaches the outskirts of Roger and Brian's home town. Being on the edge of town the two friends sitting so close to the slightly open sliding wooden door have a good view. They see their hometown all lit up and it is bright and colourful, but close to them are big metal buildings which they know are shops in a retail park. This retail park is lit up by many bright colourful shop signs, red, blue, green, yellows and any other colour that will attract people wanting to go shopping. Like big electric flowers the bright neon signs attract people like flowers attract bees. The shops here on this Friday night are busy they notice.

As the train trundles by the two friends see the big bright red, white and yellow lights of a drive-through fast food restaurant, and briefly they are close enough to smell it as they pass. On seeing this Roger feels hungry and knows that if he is hungry then Brian will definitely be hungry.

'Don't say it,' says Roger.

'Say what?' asks Brian.

'Don't say what you will go and say anyway,' explains Roger.

'I wasn't going to say anything,' insists Brian.

'You will,' mutters Roger.

They sit in silence as the train passes the fast food restaurant, getting their last whiff of hot food.

'I'm hungry,' says Brian.

'That's it! You said it!'

'What?'

'I knew you would say you're hungry,' complains Roger.

He really wishes his friend would not mention feeling hungry, here they are stuck on this moving freight train till morning and there definitely is no chance of a decent meal. For the two friends it will be a long night with empty stomachs.

'Well I am hungry,' Brian asserts.

But within a minute or so the drive-through fast food restaurant is beyond view as are the lights of all the other shops. The freight train along with its ratty passengers are left in darkness, if it was not for the small stub of candle used by the domino players in the far corner the darkness would be total. The small stub of candle however gives off so little light that most passengers in the boxcar are hidden by shadows in the dark.

The train now is passing through the countryside and the inky blackness of night is not lit by bright lights like the town they have left behind. The occasional streetlight casts a gloomy shadow whenever their freight train passes a village but otherwise they travel in complete darkness.

Roger and Brian like all rats have fairly good eyesight at night but even this is too dark for them. They are unable to see anything of the view through the gap in the open sliding door, at best everything is in silhouette. Just shadows and outlines of things can be seen and the domino players have the only light but this is only just bright enough even for them.

Through the Night

With nothing to do the two friends begin to look around the boxcar to see what the other passengers are doing to while away the journey.

The mother rat and her two children have snuggled up together and have already fallen asleep and despite the clanking and rocking of this draughty freight train Roger and Brian see this as a happy scene. Looking further they see the lone travelling rats have even settled down and gone to sleep, only they and the domino players are still awake.

Roger makes a decision, gathering together many loose strands of straw from the wooden floor of the boxcar he begins making a bed for himself and Brian so they can be reasonably comfortable.

'Might as well sleep,' he suggests.

'Yes, I'm tired anyway,' admits Brian.

Brian pulls his hood up over his head and makes himself quite comfortable on the bed of straw while Roger fidgets in his baggy red sweatshirt on the straw beside him. Enjoying the rare opportunity of fresh air the two friends choose to sleep close to the open sliding wooden door.

'Night, Rog.'

'Night, Brian.'

Within minutes after such a long, busy and eventful day the two friends are soon lulled to sleep by the gentle rhythmic rocking of the freight train.

Only the domino playing rats sitting in the corner are awake now, happily and without too much noise they keep playing and with no sign of tiring.

'Time for tea I think,' the rat in the brown raincoat suggests.

'Again? Why not?' responds a furry brown rat in a blue boiler suit and a bright, colourful woolly hat.

Another dressed much the same only with a flat cap looks up with interest at the mention of tea.

'Yeah, I'm thirsty,' he adds.

'You're always thirsty,' the rat in black remarks.

'Yeah, true. I like tea!' he explains.

This time the domino players stop their game while they sit and enjoy their cups of tea, instead they chat idly.

'What time do we get to London?' asks the woolly hat.

'6.30,' the brown raincoat replies.

'7 o'clock,' the rat in black corrects.

'I thought it was gone 8 o'clock when we arrive,' the rat in the flat cap adds.

'No, never that late,' says the rat in black.

'Not usually anyway,' adds the brown raincoat.

'Quite early though?' the woolly hat asks.

'Yeah, early enough,' the flat cap answers.

Soon enough the domino players return to their game, fuelled by many cups of tea they still have not tired of playing and seem quite fresh and wide awake.

'Right here we go. Who's got the double six?' asks the brown raincoat.

'Me,' the woolly hat replies.

'You start then,' adds the brown raincoat.

While these merry games of dominoes are being played the train trundles through the countryside and through the night. Slowly the scenery changes but it is still so dark little can be seen. No one not even the lively domino players can see the lush green fields or the gentle rolling hills in the distance. Nor can they see the fields of wheat still green but tall, growing ready for harvest time.

The freight train passes cooling towers, these are big fat chimneys belching smoke from making electricity and they are almost in darkness except for the streetlights surrounding the place. The smell of smoke and coal gives a clue to the presence of these cooling towers even to the rats sitting in the corner playing dominoes.

'Ah, Didcot,' the rat in black remarks as he sniffs the air with his long whiskery nose twitching as he draws in the familiar smells.

'Time flies when you're drinking tea,' the woolly hat remarks.

After several hours the open countryside is steadily being replaced by signs of people and their busy lives. First the long train with its freight and rats on board creaks and rattles alongside quiet villages in the barely lit middle of nowhere. Next the freight train steadily passes through small towns, many with pretty red brick houses and some with small neat modern homes so close to the railway track.

On the River Thames where it gently winds a little is a very grand white house which is set back slightly from the river bank. It is a beautiful and rather stately place, a house so grand one could imagine great balls and elegant parties being held full of beautiful and rich people. Waking briefly Brian opens his eyes and sees this grand white house almost glowing in the darkness with the moonlight shining off its white walls. Then he closes his eyes again, he believes wrongly he is dreaming.

By now even the domino players are all fast asleep, the small stub of candle they brewed tea with and saw to play by has long since been blown out.

Eventually the slow moving freight train reaches the towns that are on the outskirts of London. Slowly the sun rises and the inky blackness of night is replaced by the deep dark blue sky of twilight, the beginning of dawn, not yet day but no longer night. Now in this very dull light the freight train rolls creaking and clanking over a very elegant bridge that spans the river Thames which here has grown quite wide.

Saturday – Journey's End

After a fairly good night's sleep Roger and Brian wake up, and enjoying the dim early light of dawn, the two friends sit quietly. They are happily watching as the scenery from the gap through the sliding door constantly changes. Because they love travel and because they are always curious the two friends try reading the signs telling the name and place of the stations, but from a moving train this is not easy. Fortunately being on a freight train that moves slower than a passenger train they do not need to crick their necks too much but reading these signs are still difficult.

By now the sun has risen and the train moves onward through daylight and everything including the station signs are easier to see, if not to read.

'Did you see it Rog? Where are we?' asks Brian.

'No, sorry, I missed it. We'll try reading one at the next station,' answers Roger.

Freight trains roll along much slower than passenger trains which hurtle along at great speed. Despite this Roger and Brian sitting down at the gap in the sliding door have a problem reading the station names as the train trundles over the railway line.

Several more stations are passed through before they can discover where they are so far on their journey to London.

'West Drayton. That's where we are Brian!' reads Roger, finally.

'Oh good, well done Rog! How much further?' asks Brian.

'I don't know. But… ' Roger begins carefully.

'Go on.'

'Well, we just look out for something that looks like London and we'll know we are nearly there,' Roger suggests.

'Do you mean a big red bus, a black taxi or an underground train?' asks Brian.

'Yeah, them sort of things,' agrees Roger.

After passing this small and quite neat station what little greenery of the countryside that is left is rapidly replaced by signs of an approaching city.

Firstly the steep embankments either side of the two railway lines disappear, here the land becomes flat and is now covered by many more rail tracks. Most of these tracks are empty but some have a few unused and forgotten looking wagons for freight parked on them. One or two look just like the wooden boxcar they are all riding in on their journey to London.

Further along the track there are unused and possibly unwanted passenger carriages standing in the sidings. They look so cold, dark and empty. It is hard to imagine people once ever queued to get onboard. Now they look as though they have been left to rot.

'Those look so cold and horrible don't they,' says Brian.

'Yeah, I'm glad we're here,' admits Roger.

'Freight is great, eh Rog?' jokes Brian.

'Oh well, jokes before breakfast,' mutters Roger.

'What is breakfast? I mean when or where is breakfast?' asks Brian.

'To be honest Brian, I have no idea,' Roger admits.

After a long journey on a draughty old freight train through the night Roger and Brian are beginning to feel very hungry. They might be going to London for a statue but as soon as they arrive finding food will be the first thing the two friends will need to do.

'I'm starving,' complains Brian.

'I'm hungry too,' admits Roger.

They dwell on the serious thought of where in London they are going to eat while they watch the ever changing scenery become steadily more built up. Though now more concerned with food the two friends enjoy watching as they get closer to London the capital of England.

They are soon filled with a sense of excitement as they see the first signs of London approaching and a big red bus comes into view quickly followed by an underground train buzzing and humming along another track.

'We're nearly there!' Roger exclaims.

'Good, eat food then explore,' Brian responds.

'And find a statue,' adds Roger.

By now the other passengers in the boxcar begin stirring from their night's sleep and with surprising quickness they are soon wide awake and preparing for the end of the journey.

The mother with her two little rats wake up and being so young and full of life they are soon being a noisy handful causing their mother to work hard at getting them ready for when the train arrives. They are full of excitement, naturally they are eager to see London and growing impatient to leave the train.

'Are we there yet?' asks one.

'No, not yet,' replies the mother.

'When will we be?' asks the other.

'Soon,' replies the mother.

'How soon?' asks the first.

'Very soon,' the mother answers.

While sitting and watching the scenery Roger and Brian listen to this conversation somewhere behind them, though grown up they share the little rats' sense of excitement and even their impatience, if only because they are both so hungry.

Next to awaken are the lone travelling rats who quietly greet each other with polite "Good mornings" while they slowly get ready and freshen themselves up as best they can on the wooden floor of a straw covered boxcar.

Only the domino players are still asleep now and neither one is showing the faintest sign of waking up, there is no stirring from any one of them. Just silence from most, the occasional snore from one and a strange whistle from another. These sounds and their chests going up and down being the only signs of life from this group who for a long time through the night were full of energy. Now they are all fast asleep near their journey's end. All the other rats being awake look at the sleeping group with curiosity.

London is getting very close now, high-rise flats and Underground train stations have been passed in the last few minutes. All the rats look at each other wondering whether to wake the domino players up. It would be unkind to let them miss their destination, on the other hand the train will be at the end of the line and probably be stationary for hours…

'Do you think we should wake them?' asks one lone traveller.

'I suppose we should,' replies another.

'Be a shame to miss London,' adds the mother.

'We'll wake them!' her children yell.

In their excitement they both yell so loudly that one of the rats stirs from his sleep and all the other rats watch in silence until he returns to his deep slumbers.

'No. Leave them in peace,' warns the mother.

After several minutes of still wondering whether to wake them or not finally the slow moving freight train grinds to a halt just short of reaching Paddington station. Now out of kindness and a desire to take action Brian gets up to wake the domino players who the night before had happily supplied all on board with cups of tea. On reaching where they lay sleeping Brian sees a notice. It reads "Do not disturb. Thank you".

'Oh well, let them be. They know what they're doing,' responds Brian.

'Yes, I get the feeling they do this journey often,' Roger remarks.

Now confident that it is not rude and inconsiderate to leave the domino players on the train sleeping all the others quickly begin leaving the train. With the usual impatience of anyone at the end of a journey one of the lone rats dashes to the gap in the sliding door and quickly peers round. He looks towards the front of the freight train where the engine and its driver will be and sees the man in his overalls slowly climb down from the engine and quietly walk away.

'It's alright,' he announces, 'the driver's gone. We can leave now,' he adds.

'Can we? Great!' another lone rat says.

Suddenly all the lone rats hurriedly leave the train and such is their impatience no sooner have they descended onto the tracks than they have quickly disappeared from view.

'They didn't hang about,' observes Brian.

'Can someone help me, please?' the mother asks, politely.

Roger and Brian turn around and see the mother standing with her two young little rats holding her paws, they need help getting down from the train. Like the night before helping them aboard the two friends happily help them to leave the train.

Once they set foot on the gravel by the shiny metal tracks the two young rats become very excitable and talkative.

'Now you don't run away. We have to be very careful, big trains move around here,' the mother warns.

'Where are we going first?'

'Can we see Trafalgar Square please? Go on, please?'

Quickly though their voices fade away as their mother leads them away to safety and deeper into London.

Roger and Brian step down from the train and stand still looking around at their unfamiliar surroundings, they are wondering which way to go and more importantly where they can find a nice breakfast.

Arrival

'Well Brian… Any ideas?' asks Roger.

Brian turns and looks around just simply hoping to see somewhere offering nice tasty food. But nowhere does he see an opportunity to sit down, relax and above all have their first meal since leaving their home town the night before.

'No, I'm afraid not,' concedes Brian.

'Me neither. I wish we brought food with us,' confesses Roger.

'Well I suppose we might as well head towards the train station,' suggests Brian.

The two friends begin walking and with empty, growling stomachs they breathe in the cool fresh morning air. After a night of travel being at Paddington station fills them with a sense of excitement, they are at last in London. Once they have eaten they can begin their search for the statue of Nelson on his column and hopefully even enjoy their visit to the capital of England. But until they have fed the quest will have to wait.

The Leaky Lewis is a narrow boat, it is a traditional style of narrow boat with little round porthole windows and very pretty ornate paintwork. It is mostly black with fancy patterns in red, yellow, blue and green. There is even a pot plant with pretty red flowers growing on the roof of the Leaky Lewis. The man standing at the back steering the Leaky Lewis looks very relaxed as this narrow boat glides by gently on the water of the canal. But what leaves the biggest impression on Roger and

Brian is the slow and gentle chug chug chug chug of the narrow boat's engine.

'We are in London, aren't we?' asks Brian.

The two friends are indeed in London, they have found themselves a nice place to sit and eat near the train station called Little Venice. This is a nice quiet stretch of canal which is a man-made river. It has slow flowing water and is surrounded by trees, plants and flowers and lined with cafes and pubs along the footpath.

'Yeah mate, it's the Grand Union Canal,' a local rat responds to Brian's overheard question, he is a large but friendly looking rat taking a walk along the edge of the footpath close to the water's edge.

'We come here often, it is so pretty and peaceful,' his partner adds. She is much smaller and almost in his shadow as she holds his paw.

'It's very nice,' says Roger.

'It's called Little Venice,' the local rat explains.

'Because of the canals, and being such pretty scenery,' his partner adds. She smiles then says, 'anyway must go, bye!'

Finding themselves alone Roger and Brian sit in silence simply relaxing and enjoying the peaceful scenery of the canal. Not that the two friends know London very well, they realize that such a quiet corner in London is quite unusual.

'Lucky to find this place,' Roger notes.

'Very lucky. I didn't know this place was here,' Brian admits.

'Nor me,' adds Roger.

After such a long journey through the night on board a freight train, fresh air and pretty peaceful scenery beside water is a welcome change, especially before they return to their quest in the busy heart of London.

Now at last they have finally eaten a decent meal and are feeling refreshed and full.

The two friends are standing outside the high red brick wall of a hospital not far from Paddington station, they are close to the busy road and people going back and forth seem not to notice them. On the other side of the road are shops, cafés and a pub. There is so much to see and they soak up the atmosphere while wondering where to go next.

'It's nice being in London,' sighs Roger cheerfully. With a meal inside him he is beginning to like being here and he, like

Brian, is feeling happy. Steadily they both feel ready to take on the task dumped upon them by their Chair-rat Jeremy Brown.

'Yeah, it's sort of a working holiday, really,' agrees Brian.

'Well, where do we start?' asks Roger.

Brian falls silent a moment before deciding to answer his friend's question, they wish to enjoy their quest as much as possible and not run around aimlessly.

'Well we should see the sights, I think. Be fun as well,' suggests Brian.

Brian is determined to enjoy himself as much as possible and yet he knows they cannot really return without completing the quest for the column. If he was to be honest about it he would admit to being a little bit worried about finding this statue.

'Why not Brian and if this statue of Nelson with his column is famous we might come across it on our travels,' agrees Roger, hopefully.

'Yes, we might!' Brian shares his hope.

'But where to start…?' mutters Roger.

The two friends still standing outside the hospital look up and down the road wondering which way to go, it is doing this that supplies Roger with an idea.

He sees a sign, a red circle with a blue line through it saying Underground. It is a sign outside a London Underground station, a way for very many people to travel almost anywhere in London with ease.

'Brian, let's use the human underground,' suggests Roger.

'What? You mean the London Underground?' asks Brian, a little shocked.

'Yeah!'

Despite his friend's shock at such a suggestion he is pleased with his own idea.

'The tube?' pursues Brian.

'Yeah.'

'Those busy trains crowded with people?' asks Brian, doubtful.

'Er… Yeah. It's like the Rats Underground only quicker,' explains Roger.

'Oh, yeah, ok. Let's do it!' agrees Brian, finally.

It is difficult and even a little bit dangerous but they manage not to get trodden on or even noticed reaching the platform of the Underground station. Now Roger and Brian are standing very close to the doors on a quick-moving Underground train. The two friends are holding on tightly while the train rocks and rolls occasionally as it speeds through the dark tunnels on electric rails. It is a crowded train and they are surrounded by a forest of legs of the people who, like themselves, have no seat. Like them they are standing waiting for the train to reach their station.

At the first few stations where the train stops the two friends decide to stay on board thinking perhaps they are not near enough to the centre of London. Instead they just watch as the now moving forest of legs leave the train, making way for more people to step on board. Roger and Brian see all this and press themselves tightly out of reach in fear of getting squashed. Then the train which by now is hot and stuffy carries on its journey through the dark tunnels to the next stations.

Roger and Brian are now wishing they were back up on the surface breathing fresh air and feeling the cool breeze. They decide it is time to leave the train, now fortunately they reach another station on the London Underground.

'Where are we?' asks Roger.

'Who cares? Let's get out,' Brian answers, almost breathless. He can no longer bear the heat and the crowds down here, the Rats Underground is never this bad. Down there instead it is often cold and draughty, though also smelly. Brian longs for the dark, damp peace of the R.U. rather than this brightly lit and very crowded place.

They hurriedly leave the train among the legs of the tightly packed crowd of people while trying not to get trodden on and not wishing to get hurt they even carry their tails. Walking along the two friends get a brief glance of an Underground sign, it says "Oxford Circus".

'That's where we are!' exclaims Brian.

'Yes, I wonder what's there… Any idea Brian?'

'No, not a clue, one way to find out though.' answers Brian.

'We'll follow these people out as quickly as we can and then we'll find out,' suggests Roger.

Eventually after much walking in tunnels and riding on escalators they manage to leave the station and breathe a sigh of relief to be outside once again. This is where they hope now to escape from the huge crowds of people but Roger and Brian soon discover though that even here the place is very busy.

They step into Oxford Circus and are amazed and a little bit frightened by the sight of so many people in one place. Being rats and so little, the people to them are not much more than a swirling mass of moving legs and feet. They have seen crowds before but never this many where people are packed so closely together. The slow moving mass of people however give Roger an idea, he realizes they are really quite safe out here in the open even among so many people. It is so busy that even if anyone did notice them they would not be very bothered about a pair of rats.

'Hey Brian, if we're quick we can dodge through their legs,' suggests Roger.

'Oh well, ok, at least they are barely moving. Come on then,' agrees Brian, nervously.

The two friends run quickly darting through and between the legs of the people who are sightseeing and shopping and it is with much effort that they reach the kerb. As they do a big red bus pulls up beside them and without hesitating Roger and Brian quickly leap on board. For the moment at least they can relax.

They stand on the open platform of the big red bus as it moves slowly along the road among the heavy traffic which crawls along. From here they see the shoppers and the many different shops as they pass very slowly along Oxford Street.

'It's a busy place,' notes Brian.

'Very,' agrees Roger.

'Do you think it's always like this?' asks Brian.

'Surely not. That would be mad!' suggests Roger.

Riding on the bus the two friends stand near the edge of the platform holding on tight to the pole for fear of falling. They stare in amazement at the heaving crowds as they slowly shuffle along the pavement. Also they admire the scenery with big elegant buildings standing tall towering over them and the many people here. The buildings look so solid and proud and with bright colourful lights glowing even in daylight attracting the shoppers.

'I heard once that it's really good along here at Christmas,' says Brian.

'Good?'

'Yeah, all lit up nicely with decorations. And even busier!' answers Brian.

Escaping the Crowds

A little further along the bus reaches Hyde Park Corner. Seeing the wide open space with fields of grass dotted with several trees Roger and Brian realize they feel a need for peace and quiet, they wish to escape the chaos that surrounds them. As soon as the bus stops Roger and Brian enter the safety and the peace of the park as quickly as their little legs can carry them. They do not wish to leave the city they have come to visit but they are both already beginning to feel worn out by the excitement of the place.

Reaching the park Roger and Brian breathe a sigh of relief and walk along slowly enjoying the wide open spaces, here they almost feel at home.

'Much better,' sighs Roger.

'Do we have to face them crowds again, do you think?' asks Brian.

'Probably,' admits Roger.

'Well the Chair-rat had better be grateful,' responds Brian.

Once in the park Roger and Brian do not stop, instead they keep on walking until they reach a quiet area with tables and chairs beneath a large tree. Just beyond here they discover they are not the only rats in the park. To their surprise they see a rat in orange overalls sweeping up close to a litter bin.

'Excuse me!' calls Roger.

The rat in orange overalls looks up briefly but carries on sweeping despite being called.

'Can you tell me where to find Nelson's Column?' asks Roger.

'Yeah, it's in London innit,' the sweeper answers unhelpfully.

'No I mean where in London?'

Roger's words tail off to a mutter when he realizes the sweeping rat is paying no attention to his questions or to either himself or Brian. Roger knows he is wasting his time talking to this rat who is more concerned with his job of sweeping, he barely even notices them standing there. Not wishing to waste any more of their time Roger and Brian leave him to his work and move on through the park hoping for better luck.

After much walking the two friends reach the Serpentine which is a famous lake in Hyde Park, seeing this nice lake they both decide here will be a very nice place to stay a while and have a rest.

Finding themselves a nice spot they lie down on their backs resting on the grass listening to the birds singing and hearing the traffic in the not too far distance. But while laying on their backs they look up and watch the clouds rolling by in the blue sky.

'That cloud looks like a cat,' observes Brian.

A round cloud which appears to have two triangular pointed ears is above them, very briefly it even seems to have whiskers, but these soon disappear as the cloud moves through the sky.

'Oh yeah! And that one looks like a car,' replies Roger.

Another long thin cloud glides by and for a very short moment it looks like a sleek fast sports car.

By watching clouds Roger and Brian manage to keep themselves amused while having a nice rest. But still they wonder where they will find Nelson's Column.

Eventually Roger and Brian feel fully rested and also bored with watching clouds so they get up off the grass, dust themselves down and take a stroll around this nice lake called the Serpentine.

'Well, any ideas?' asks Roger.

'What? Where to find a meal?' asks Brian.

'No, how we're going to find Nelson's Column.'

'Oh that,' responds Brian.

'Yes, that,' Roger replies.

'I do have one idea,' says Brian.

'Which is?' asks Roger.

'We can ask him,' explains Brian.

They see a rat hitching a ride on the back of a dustcart which is moving slowly through the park collecting rubbish. The man driving the dustcart they guess is not going to stop and seizing the opportunity Brian quickly asks his question.

'Where can we find Nelson's Column?' he calls.

'In London,' the hitch hiking rat replies, quickly.

'No I meant… Oh never mind,' groans Brian.

Roger and Brian are stuck for ideas, now they do not know where to go, nor do they really know what to do next, so they just keep on walking along through the park. Shortly after leaving the lake behind them the sound of traffic steadily becomes louder until the busy noises of the city disturb their quiet walk.

The two friends are close to an open gate leading out of Hyde Park and beyond they can see signs of noisy, busy London. Already they can even smell the fumes coming from the slow-moving traffic crawling along the crowded road outside the park.

In front of them inside the park they see a rat in an ill-fitting black pin-striped suit carrying a wooden walking stick.

This rat has grey fur showing on his bare feet, head and on his paws while his long pink tail drags behind him along the ground. Strangely this rat is moving back and forth by a bush close to the open gate, whether he is looking for something Roger and Brian cannot tell. But seeing another rat and one that probably lives here gives Roger an idea and seizing the opportunity he quickly approaches the smartly dressed rat.

'Excuse me, where does this lead to?' asks Roger, pointing through the gate.

The rat in the black pin-striped suit stops doing whatever it is he is doing among the bushes and looks in the direction of Roger's pointed finger.

'Knightsbridge dear boy!' he answers.

'Knightsbridge?' repeats Brian.

'Yes. Posh London, very rich,' the pin striped rat replies.

'Do you know where Nelson's Column is?' asks Brian, getting to the point quickly.

The rat in the black pin-striped suit stops for a moment and gives the question some thought. He rubs his furry chin with his paw while he thinks. Suddenly his eyes light up and this fills Roger and Brian with a great sense of hope, at last they think we are on our way to getting this statue and going home. With such hope they wait for the pin-striped rat's answer.

'Why yes, I think I do!' he replies.

But before they can pursue their question any further the grey rat in the pin-striped suit carrying his wooden walking stick turns and walks away with surprising speed. So sudden and so quick does he move that Roger and Brian only just see him disappear into the bush. They try following him but it is no use, they cannot find where he went.

'Great!' moans Brian, thinking it is anything but great.

'That's the closest we've come to finding our answer,' says Roger.

Feeling disheartened he sits down on a stone.

'I know and we've been in London for hours,' complains Brian.

'Spoken to several rats…' notes Roger.

'And only had stupid answers,' adds Brian.

Understandably poor Roger and Brian are beginning to feel frustrated, they have been trying so hard to find this statue for their Chair-rat and they dare not return without it. Yet since before they even left home they have had so many problems, from being chased by people and now getting silly answers to simple questions. Worse still, it is beginning to get dark as night approaches and the two friends realize they will have to stay in London overnight.

'Oh well, might as well enter Knightsbridge,' says Roger standing up.

Knightsbridge and Biscuit Tins

The two friends leave Hyde Park behind them and step for the first time into Knightsbridge. After the jam packed crowds of Oxford Street they are relieved to see that though it is very busy they do not have to deal with heaving crowds and a forest of legs. There are plenty of people here but they can still see plenty of empty pavement.

'Room to breathe, that's a relief!' says Roger.

'Yes, that was too crowded and busy earlier, I didn't like it,' replies Brian.

'Me neither,' admits Roger.

As they walk along the busy road in Knightsbridge the light fades on what for Roger and Brian has been an unsuccessful day. They are here now in a posh part of London and they look up in awe at the very grand buildings that tower over them. It seems to them that this place was once built by proud and very important people with lots of money. Roger and Brian look around at the scenery and the people shopping and feel they do not belong here. They hope no one notices them and if they are seen, hopefully they will be considered as tourists and not invaders.

'Do you think rats live here Rog?' asks Brian.

'Rats live everywhere,' answers Roger.

'I haven't seen any since leaving the park and it's so posh here,' notes Brian.

'Us rats are good at many things Brian but there are two things that matter,' says Roger.

'Which is?'

'We can live anywhere we choose and we usually manage to keep out of sight,' answers Roger.

'True, very true,' agrees Brian.

'Rats live here, they're just hidden away somewhere, that's all,' adds Roger.

Still walking the two friends see the occasional building that they know as famous. These are things they have seen in pictures or simply heard about which end up as part of a tourist trail. Even they stop occasionally to have a good long look before moving on, but seeing such sights causes Roger to wonder.

'Hey Brian, I just thought. How big is this Nelson's Column?'

'Ah... Well... it can't be that big,' answers Brian, 'or else the Chair-rat wouldn't have sent us to get it.'

'That's true as it wouldn't fit in the R.U. if it was too big anyway,' agrees Roger.

A big round red brick building with tall windows appears in their view. It seems to have about four layers with a very big, very grand entrance and a domed roof. The lower half has tall narrow windows while the next layer has tall arched windows. Above this is a balcony running all the way round and above this is a frieze. It is is a band which runs around the building and this one is creamy in colour but pretty and very detailed with pictures of people doing various different things.

'That's the Royal Albert Hall,' Roger explains.

He stands pointing up at this pretty building as though he is a tour guide and appears ready to tell his tourist, Brian more about the place.

'It looks like a fancy biscuit tin to me,' replies Brian, slightly unimpressed.

'I always know when you're hungry,' says Roger.

'It does! Look, there's the fancy pattern around the top and the roof is the lid. Inside are the biscuits just waiting to be dunked into a nice hot cup of tea,' Brian replies, with enthusiasm.

'Ah tea, good idea, pity we don't have any with us,' Roger sighs.

Both realize they could do with a refreshing drink, it has been hours since breakfast but with no tea and not knowing where to get a cup of tea they just keep walking. Leaving the Royal Albert Hall behind they keep going but they do not really know where to go next. The two friends hope to see some sign or clue which may lead them to Nelson's Column. As they are here in London they might as well take in the scenery and enjoy a bit of sightseeing, after all it would be a wasted opportunity not to see things you would only read about or see in pictures.

It is with this thought in mind they suddenly find their attention is grabbed by the biggest, grandest corner shop they have ever seen. It is a shop that goes up covering many floors and is housed in a beautiful, elegant building, it even has royal crests resting proudly over the main entrance on the corner of the building. One for the Queen, one for the Prince of Wales...

Roger and Brian are hugely impressed by such a grand sight and so they think are the many people that are entering or leaving through the busy doors.

'I'd love to shop there,' admits Roger.

'Me too, I wonder what it's like inside?' replies Brian.

'Yeah... I'm not going in though, I've had enough of being chased lately,' Roger says, after a thought.

'Oh yeah, pity, never mind,' Brian agrees.

Wisely they stay outside and stare in awe at this very grand and probably expensive shop and try to imagine what it must be like inside. Despite their difficult quest and their lack of success today they are beginning to enjoy themselves in London.

Walking further along Roger and Brian see the entrance to a very crowded, busy Underground station. They recognise it by the familiar red circle with the blue line going left to right through the middle and this reminds them of the Rats Underground logo. Which as they know is a yellow R with a yellow U below and slightly to the right within a blue circle.

'Our sign for the R.U. is better,' says Brian.

'Very true, but theirs isn't bad,' replies Roger.

They see all these people packed close together moving slowly around the entrance of the Underground station, few people seem to be emerging but many are entering.

'I wonder where they are going?' thinks Roger, out loud.

'I don't know, let's find out, lets follow them,' suggests Brian.

Brian is not normally an impulsive rat, suddenly having an idea and quickly deciding to act upon it is out of character for him. He usually likes to take his time and think about things first. Unless of course it is about food then Brian can be very quick making his mind up, so naturally his friend Roger is surprised.

Being surprised Brian is so eager to follow a heaving crowd of people Roger looks at him in sheer amazement and sees by the look on his friend's face he is serious.

'Ok, why not?' agrees Roger.

On agreeing to such a quick decision the two friends follow the packed crowd of people down into the Underground station at Knightsbridge. Roger and Brian manage to weave between the legs of all these people stepping carefully onto the escalator. Once this moving staircase reaches the bottom they quickly step off and follow the crowds. Most they notice are heading towards the "Eastbound" platform.

'Let's go that way,' says Brian.

'Yeah, might as well,' agrees Roger.

'I wonder where it leads, did you read the sign?' asks Brian. 'No, but we'll soon find out though,' answers Roger.

People are usually so wrapped up in their own lives, thinking about their problems or what they have to do next they simply miss things that are around them. Roger and Brian rely on this, hoping as often, not to be noticed when out and about among people. The library incident has made them both nervous and they try to be more careful and hope to be more lucky. Cautiously they are standing on the crowded platform at Knightsbridge waiting for the next train. They stand well back from the edge because when the train appears it can cause a shockwave of air which can blow them off their feet, even the people they notice stand back. They look towards the tunnel when they feel a warm gust of air come from that way, still looking they then hear a distant rumble. Everyone around them start moving about expecting something. It is, of course, why everyone here is waiting.

From the darkness of the tunnel the train emerges and in less than a minute the train races past the platform right in front of them. The two friends can see the passengers through the windows of the train that is all lit up from within. The white train slows down to a halt and then its red doors slide open allowing passengers off and on. Now Roger and Brian quickly hop aboard hidden among people's legs. The doors slide shut and the train pulls away again ending its brief visit to the platform.

As the train whizzes through the dark tunnels it rocks a little from side to side making the passengers standing up hold on tightly. Not being able to hold onto a handrail Roger and Brian keep their balance by planting their hairy bare feet firmly on the floor and leaning against the side by the door. It is hot and stuffy inside this train and Brian has his hood down, but even so he is still hot. Roger has taken his baggy red sweatshirt off and tied it around his waist. Wearing his pale blue T-shirt with RAT in dark blue letters Roger leans impatiently in the train wishing it would stop so they can get off. They have managed to stay on for the last two stops but have had enough of riding on the human underground now. They do not really know where they are going and they are too low to see out of the train windows which is only useful when a train reaches a station anyway, so they are hoping for a little bit of good luck.

'I prefer the Rats Underground!' calls Roger. He shouts above the roar and the rattle of the train as it hums and whizzes through the dark tunnel.

'Me too!' admits Brian.

'Shall we get off at the next station?' asks Roger.

'Yes! Definitely!' Brian continues, 'Where shall that be?'

As Brian finishes asking this question the speeding train brakes slowing them down ready to stop at the platform of the next Underground station.

'We are at... Piccadilly Circus.' answers Roger.

It is only as the doors open does he see the Underground sign that declares at which station they have arrived.

'Oh good, I've heard about this one,' says Brian.

'How do you know this place?' asks Roger, surprised.

'I do read books... Well I look at the pictures mostly,' answers Brian, honestly.

'Well that's good Brian. What's here then?' asks Roger, impressed with his friend.

By now the two friends have stepped off the train and are carefully moving along with the crowds of people. Some people are making their way to catch another train but most are heading towards the escalator which leads to the street above and these the two friends quickly follow.

Piccadilly Circus

Two rats are walking along in Piccadilly Circus Underground station. One is feeling hot in his blue jeans and hooded blue top while he walks along with his hood down. The other is in his brown corduroy trousers wearing his baggy red sweatshirt tied around his waist which earlier covered his pale blue RAT T-shirt.

These two rats weaving through the legs of people leaving the station should be easily noticed but people in a hurry as Roger and Brian know well notice very little.

'Well?' asks Roger.

'Well what?' asks Brian.

'Well, what's here?' asks Roger.

'Ah well, wait and see,' replies Brian.

Standing at the feet of many people the two friends step off the escalator and take the last few steps through the station. Now they pass through the gates where people have to stop and scan their tickets and here they leave people standing as they pass easily under the gate. There is only a short walk to the steps which lead up to the street above.

'We're nearly there. Here we go...' announces Brian.

They climb up off the last few stone steps leading into the street above where for the first time they see the famous sights here.

'Eros!' Brian declares.

It is night time now though the black sky is mostly hidden by tall buildings, street lights and the famous attractions. The night arrived in London shortly before Roger and Brian arrived here in Piccadilly Circus but now they see everything is lit up so well.

As planned by Brian they reach the surface into the street beside Eros, this is the well-known Cupid-like statue of a man with wings holding a bow. Many people, shoppers and tourists are here and some are sitting by Eros.

'See that statue, it's Eros. Very nice, don't you think?' says Brian.

'Yeah, very. So if this is Eros it's not Nelson's Column?' asks Roger.

'No, we're still yet to find that,' admits Brian.

'Oh well,' mutters Roger.

Losing interest in Eros he quickly turns around and sees for the first time what Brian kept as a surprise about Piccadilly Circus. Being a rat used to his West Country storm drain home on the Rats Underground Roger is now standing silent and filled with amazement at what he can see.

Across the road completely covering one whole corner of a building is a huge sign that wraps smoothly around top to bottom. It is a collection of adverts for many different things people use everyday, whether it is drinks or electrical items or something else. But this sign is special because all these things are advertised in bright colourful lights, it is an impressive sight and one much enjoyed by tourists and rats alike.

'What a sight! What an amazing sight! Look at that Brian,' declares an excitable Roger.

'It's good eh?' agrees Brian.

'You knew about this place?' asks Roger.

'Yeah, you like it then?' asks Brian.

'It's incredible!' says Roger.

The two friends are standing together staring up in amazement, now they are truly enjoying their visit to London even though it was forced upon them.

Standing here at night looking at all the bright lights and pretty buildings while seeing the traffic passing by Roger and Brian now realize why London is such a popular place to visit. They decide to forget about their quest for the rest of the night, after all they are cheerful enough to believe that somehow a solution to their problem will be found.

With this thought in mind they decide to spend the rest of the night having a little bit of fun in the capital of England.

'What do you think Rog? I think it would be nice to see more of London,' Brian suggests.

'Be tourists? Yeah, why not? That would be nice,' agrees Roger.

'Yeah, the Chair-rat never said we couldn't enjoy ourselves,' says Brian.

'No, he didn't,' Roger replies.

The two friends stand silently, simply enjoying being here watching the world busily go by among all the bright lights of Piccadilly Circus.

'So… What shall we do then?' asks Brian.

A big red double-decker bus appears slowly moving its way through the busy traffic and where they are standing close to Eros, Roger and Brian can see this bus. This is a big red bus with adverts on its side and its windows all lit up top and bottom glowing pale yellow under the black night sky. The appearance of this big red bus adds to the chaotic but lively scene the two friends and everyone else here is enjoying. They see the front of this bus and read the destination sign which appeals to Roger greatly.

'Hey look!' he says, pointing excitably at the bus, 'I want to go there.'

'Ok let's hop on this bus, it's easy when the back is open,' replies Brian.

Doing their best to ignore the crowds of people gathered close to the statue of Eros the two friends quickly run towards the big red bus which fortunately has had to stop because of the slow-moving traffic. Roger and Brian climb on board at the open end of the bus at the back and carefully hold onto the handrail which is a pole that divides the open doorway into two. Ready they wait for the bus to begin moving again and when it does they find they have a great slow changing view of London and its famous sights. All is lit up so colourfully and the buildings so elegant and pretty. What with many other big red double-decker buses, black cabs and the busy crowds of people all milling around the place is bright, noisy and very exciting.

'Why haven't we done this before?' asks Roger

'Because we haven't been sent on a silly errand before,' Brian answers, bluntly.

'True,' admits Roger.

The Blues Bar

In Carnaby Street among one of the many shops that line this famous street is a tiny little night club. There are two reasons that this is a tiny little night club, firstly because this is a night club much enjoyed by rats seeking a good time. Secondly because this place exists beneath one of the many shops that line Carnaby Street.

This night club is simply called The Blues Bar, which is a nice easy name to remember but it also refers to the music that is often played here. In The Blues Bar live bands play blues and jazz music through the night all the way to the break of dawn. When the sun rises all the sociable music-loving rats leave the club and make their way home to their beds. But now the evening is only just beginning, The Blues Bar has opened its doors for the night and rats from all directions are already pouring through the door. Many, though not all, are regulars here, they are coming to relax in a lively but friendly place while enjoying good music in the company of other rats who like good live music.

In The Blues Bar there is a small slightly raised stage where the bands can perform, while opposite is the entrance which is a single door leading down a few steps into the club. Along the wall almost tucked into the corner close to the door is the bar while along the bare brick walls are tea lights giving just enough light into the night club. In the main area of the club covering the floor are several small round tables where many rats are sitting already having a good time watching the early part of the show.

At the door keeping the place safe and secure is a large rat dressed smartly in a black suit, plain white polo shirt and black bow tie. The smart door rat is allowing two more rats into the night club, the taller, thinner one is wearing pale blue jeans and a hooded blue top. He pulls the hood down as he enters while the other in pale brown corduroy trousers and a baggy red sweatshirt quietly follows his friend. Another smartly dressed rat leads the pair to an empty table close to the stage.

'Do you know, I'm beginning to think we were lucky to be given this quest,' says Brian.

He speaks when the music stops, they have just got themselves comfortable at their table close to the stage.

'Me too! To be honest. I'm glad we're here, it's great!' Roger keenly agrees.

'And we have a great table too,' adds Brian.

'We do, such a great view of the stage, this is going to be a good night, I think,' says Roger.

By good fortune the two friends find themselves sitting at a table enjoying live music in London, this is so different to their usual lives in a draughty storm drain. Despite being here in London seeking Nelson's Column for the Chair-rat of the Rats Underground Southwest Drains Region tonight at least Roger and Brian consider themselves on holiday.

After a brief quiet interval on the stage a new act appears to be ready to perform. Then a small slightly plump rat in a black suit, white T-shirt and crooked black bow tie walks out onto the stage smiling.

'Good evening, good evening, hello and a big hearty warm welcome to you all from us here at The Blues Bar. I'm MC Flowers, I eat flowers, tasty, yum.'

By now MC Flowers the rat in the crooked bow tie has the attention of the whole audience who are now hanging on his every word.

'I love eating flowers so that is my name.' he explains 'Anyway back to the show. Tonight we have some great music for you and we will begin with…!'

MC Flowers builds this up so the audience are stirred up and highly alert.

'Dog Bone Walker! Yesssss!' declares MC Flowers with great excitement, as he claps and cheers.

With equal excitement the audience including Roger and Brian sitting at their table clap and cheer loudly as the show begins.

On the stage walks a tall, lean and a rather scruffy rat in grubby blue jeans and a red checked long sleeved T-shirt hanging loose. Dog Bone Walker is otherwise covered in grey fur and his long pink tail drags slowly behind him as he strolls onto the stage carrying his guitar. Reaching the centre of the stage he stands ready to speak to the audience. His drummer and bass player are on the stage ready and waiting to begin but first Dog Bone Walker clearly wishes to speak to the audience. Once he is sure he has the attention of the audience he begins;

'Howdy doody! You alright? Anyway before we begin I would like to make mention of a very good friend. My friend is Sam the Strat.'

Some of the audience, the ones who come here regularly have heard of Sam the Strat, he as they know is a rat who lives at the back of a music shop nearby.

Sam the Strat uses bits and pieces out of the rubbish bins to make surprisingly good musical instruments. By finding bits of old or broken musical instruments he somehow makes things that musical rats are able to pick up and play.

'If it wasn't for him,' Dog Bone Walker adds, 'then I wouldn't be here tonight. So quickly did he build me a new guitar, so let's hear it for Sam the Strat!'

Again the audience clap and cheer while Dog Bone proudly holds his new guitar up high for all to see.

The new guitar looks quite good though it is plain, it is made from plywood and even has six metal strings. Rats are clever creatures and Sam the Strat is very clever being able to make a guitar. To make something small enough for a rat to play and on this occasion a blues-loving rat takes real skill.

Dog Bone Walker has a small group, the rest of the band are simply two rats on bass and drums. The bass is a big tall thing standing upright, really it is a double bass which looks like a huge violin and the strings are plucked by the rat's furry fingers. This also has been made from an old piece of wood and remains of old bass strings from the nearby music shop.

The drums however are made from the small size of old baked bean cans, one still has the label wrapped around it and the lids serve excellently as cymbals.

The skins covering the drums is some sort of tight fitting cloth and the drum sticks are toothpicks.

With these instruments Dog Bone Walker and his small band are ready to entertain with some good blues music.

'And now...' Dog Bone Walker announces, 'Music, the blues!'

With this he starts playing his brand new guitar and the rest of the band quickly join in.

'It's the Dirty Sewers Blues!' Dog bone Walker calls in a sing song voice and he begins singing;

"I woke up this morning
With brown things floating around my head
I said
I woke up this morning

With brown things floating around my head
It was then I knew…
I wasn't going to get out of bed
'Cos I woke up this morning
With the down the dirty sewers blues!"

Dog Bone Walker sings the Dirty Sewers Blues with great feeling, he and his band play the music with wonderful energy. The band and the audience are soon having a great time.

'He's good!' calls Roger.

'He is, he really knows our lifestyle,' agrees Brian.

'Yeah, he must have travelled the R.U.,' adds Roger.

'Most of his life I expect,' suggests Brian.

Dog Bone Walker and his small band carry on playing while Roger and Brian along with the rest of the audience in The Blues Bar enjoy watching and above all listening to their show.

It is later in the evening now, Dog Bone Walker's great show has now finished and there is an interval while the stage is quietly swept and cleared ready for the next act. Interestingly once the stage has been cleaned, for the first time tonight the curtains are drawn across the stage. Now the audience wait chatting among themselves wondering what is happening behind the big red curtains with the gold trim.

Finally they are ready for the next act and MC Flowers returns to the stage. Standing in front of the drawn big red curtains with the gold trim his appearance quickly gains the attention of the audience who stop talking among themselves.

'Hello, hello, how are you? That was good wasn't it?' MC Flowers continues, 'Now after the great Dog Bone Walker it is time for something more mellow. Something softer and more relaxing…'

MC Flowers says this to the audience in a soothing voice, he is putting the audience in the mood for mellow music.

'Now, it is time for Ellie and the Blue J's!' he announces loudly.

Once again the audience clap and cheer with great excitement, Roger and Brian are caught up in the mood of the place and happily join in. They, too, feel excited even though they have never heard of Ellie and the Blue J's but they had never heard of Dog Bone Walker and they loved his music.

The big red curtains with the gold trim are slowly drawn open revealing a pretty female rat standing in the centre of the stage smiling.

She is wearing a shiny blue dress that hugs her body displaying her female curvy rat shape while her long pink tail gently sweeps side to side as she turns and smiles at the audience. On top of her head sit's a black broad rimmed hat which covers her ears and even shades one eye so that she can see but not easily be seen. On top of this hat adding a sharp contrast to her shiny blue dress is one single juicy red strawberry.

Ellie is quite a sight on the stage in her shiny body-hugging blue dress and with her long pink tail looking clean and groomed. She smiles happily at the audience and the big black hat with its juicy strawberry on top balances with surprising ease, grace even.

Once Ellie is sure she has the attention of the whole audience and they are all looking at her she begins to speak.

'Hello. It is so good to be here tonight at The Blues Bar.' Ellie welcomes her audience while her band take their places on the stage behind her. Ellie and the Blue J's are a jazz band. Jazz is a type of music which has a free flowing easy going sound and those playing it can often do little solo performances in the middle of songs.

In this jazz band, like most jazz bands, there is a bass. This one is much like the one in Dog Bone Walker's band, a huge violin which stands upright and has the strings plucked. Of course there is a drum kit this is also like the ones used by Dog Bone Walker's drummer and these too are old baked bean cans, the small ones, not the usual large size of course. But these do not have the labels still attached, instead of the rough and ready look favoured by the blues playing rats earlier, these are smart and shiny, reflecting the light from the tea lights lining the wall of The Blues Bar. Adding a variety of sound this drum kit also has cymbals made from the lids removed from the baked bean cans which add a nice metallic sound or even a harsh crashing sound depending on the mood of the drummer.

Like a lot of jazz bands this one has a piano, though it is a mystery how this old thing was ever made. It is a rickety looking old thing and it is a wonder that it sounds as good as it does.

A clarinet is a woodwind instrument and the Blue J's have something that almost resembles one in both look and sound. This is made from a hollowed out twig and they call it a "Clarinot" because it is not a clarinet.

'Welcome to my band,' Ellie says smiling 'They're the Blue J's,' she points in their direction with an outstretched paw.

Four instruments with four rats wearing bright blue suits are waiting happily to begin playing music. One by one Ellie points to each member of the blue suited Blue J's and introduces them to the audience.

'Here we have AJ, BJ, CJ, and DJ, they're brothers,' Ellie explains.

Seeing four rats in bright blue suits with their bright pink tails trailing behind them and all with the letter J in their name it is clear how they get their name Blue J's.

'I wonder if Ellie is wearing her blue dress to match her band?' Roger asks.

'I wonder why she's got a big red strawberry on her hat?' says Brian.

After a flourish on the drums, a quick but lively little solo from the drummer and a fancy little tinkling sound from the piano the band begin playing. The band it soon appears are good, their sound unlike Dog Bone Walker's quick paced lively sound is much more mellow. Their music is slower, smoother and more relaxing.

The music Ellie and the Blue J's play is cheerful yet soothing, it is music to listen to rather than tap your foot to, something Roger and Brian quickly realize. But it is when Ellie begins singing the two friends, along with every other rat in The Blues Bar discover, that they are a really good band. Clearly Ellie is a very good entertainer, everyone admires watching the Blue J's in their bright blue suits playing their instruments enthusiastically. But more than this the audience love watching Ellie in her shiny blue dress with a juicy red strawberry on her black broad rimmed hat. From under the peak of her hat they can see her smiling as she sings, everyone feels she is smiling at them and everyone would like Ellie to join them at their table after the show.

It is just when all the rats sitting happily at their tables or standing cheerfully along the bar are thinking this could not get any better when Ellie and the Blue J's do something amazing. While playing a lively piece of music Ellie sings loudly and quickly. On the chorus she sings;

Well, I'll eat my hat!

This is the very catchy chorus to the lively song she is singing which is repeated often throughout the song.

After the third, fourth or even fifth time of singing;

Well I'll eat my hat!

The band start playing among themselves each taking a turn to do a solo spot. Firstly the clarinot, the rat version of the clarinet plays wildly going up and down the scales while reaching some very high notes. Next the piano plays a bouncy, happy rhythm which sounds like good fun to play. This is followed by the bass which makes a good thumping deep sound for a brief moment before the drummer takes over. The rat on the drums must love this bit of the show because he clearly looks to be having fun showing off his skills. He does not have a very big drum kit, just three drums and one is a bass drum laying on its side facing the audience and a cymbal but he makes it all sound huge. He bangs and crashes his way around for several minutes with great energy. Bang thud bang crash, bang crash bang crash bang bang bang, thud crash bang go his drums and cymbal. He almost stands up lifting himself off his stool in his desire to play well, and then this suddenly ends...

The solo session is over and once again the band play excitedly together and the audience clap and cheer with great joy and excitement, this was a great bit of showing off by the band.

While the band are still playing Ellie sits down and takes off her black broad rimmed hat and to the amazement of the whole audience she starts eating the juicy red strawberry.

'That's why she wears a strawberry in her hat!' exclaims Brian.

'To eat her hat,' adds Roger.

Once Ellie has finished eating her strawberry she places the leafy green stalk back on her hat before putting her hat back on her head covering her ears. Now she stands up ready to sing again.

Well I'll eat my hat
And I've ate my hat!

Sings Ellie and once again the audience applaud.

By now everyone like the Blue J's and love Ellie. The whole of The Blues Bar is almost buzzing with excitement at the sheer enjoyment of the music and the great performance.

Encore and More...

After a few more songs Ellie and the Blue J's finish playing to loud clapping and cheering from an excited and happy crowd of music-loving rats. It is several minutes before the audience even begin to calm down.

'Encore!' calls the audience.

'Encore!' calls Roger and Brian.

'What does "encore" mean?' asks Brian.

'It means once more, we want more, Brian,' answers Roger.

'Oh, I see,' says Brian.

'Encore!' the audience including Roger and Brian call loudly.

After a few more minutes and to the great delight of everyone Ellie and the Blue J's reappear on stage and decide to play once more.

But even a great show must finally come to an end and after the encore the Blue J's put down their instruments and waving to the audience they leave the stage. They disappear quickly round the back from where they appeared earlier in the evening.

Being different Ellie chooses to leave the stage but join the audience instead. Roger and Brian are amazed and even excited to see Ellie in her shiny blue dress heading their way. They would never expect to see any performer leave the stage and join the audience.

'Hey Brian, Ellie's coming this way.'

'Yeah, but she won't come to our table,' says Brian.

'She might,' says Roger.

'She won't,' says Brian.

'Why not?' asks Roger.

'Cos she won't,' Brian answers, unhelpfully.

'Are you two from the West Country?' a friendly voice asks.

This question surprises and distracts the two friends who until now were discussing whether Ellie would join them at their table. Oddly the voice is strangely familiar... The two friends look up and the first thing they see is a shiny blue dress blocking their view, on closer inspection they both realize Ellie is standing beside them at their table.

'Sorry to ask, only I recognise your accents,' Ellie apologises.

'Um...' says a dumbstruck Brian.

'Er...' says Roger, also lost for words.

Roger is the first to recover his composure, seeing Ellie standing there threw them both for a moment as neither expected the star of the show to come and speak to them.

'Yeah um, how er do you know?' Roger manages to ask.

'From there myself!' answers Ellie, almost with pride.

'Really?' asks Brian.

'What's it like there? Is it ok? Lots of green bits when I left,' asks Ellie.

'Yeah, it's ok, lots of new buildings now,' answers Brian.

'But there's still plenty of green bits,' adds Roger.

'We'd like to go back as soon as we can,' Brian admits.

'But we can't yet,' adds Roger.

'Why ever not?' Ellie asks.

By now Ellie is sitting down at the table with Roger and Brian who begin telling her their tale.

They begin right at the beginning of their adventure even mentioning the herald appearing in their storm drain home while they were still in bed. In great detail they describe visiting Jeremy Brown, the Chair-rat of the Rats Underground Southwest Drains Region in his office. And this of course leads to their quest for the column.

Roger and Brian are just about to tell Ellie of their misfortunes which even caused them to run for their lives but Ellie interrupts them.

'Column? With Nelson on?' she asks.

'Yeah?' questions Brian.

'Why? Have you heard of it?' asks Roger.

'Well, I think I might have,' admits Ellie.

Silence descends on their table, all three rats sit there quietly lost in their own thoughts. Neither know what to say next yet feel a need to speak.

'Why did you move to London?' asks Brian, changing the subject.

'To be a singer. I'm a singing rat,' replies Ellie.

'Oh right, yeah, I see,' Brian responds, feeling silly.

'The Chair-rat, you say he wants Nelson's Column in the R.U?' Ellie asks.

'Yeah, is that what it's called?' asks Brian.

'Yes.'

'Do you know where it is?' Roger asks.

He is beginning to feel excited, the two friends sense they have an opportunity to finally solve their quest.

'Well I think I do,' Ellie replies.

'Great!' exclaims Brian.

'You think?' notes Roger, with caution.

'Yes, well, meet me at the Embankment at daybreak, by the water's edge.'

Before they can respond Ellie stands up and leaves, she is gone from sight so quickly neither Roger or Brian have the chance to follow her. Instead they remain seated staring in the direction her blue dress and long pink tail are last seen by them.

The problem with daybreak is that it is so early often appearing long before it is time to get up out of bed. With this in mind Roger and Brian decide it is time to leave The Blues Bar and find themselves somewhere to spend the rest of the night and above all get some sleep. After such an eventful day they are both tired and now wish to go to sleep.

Sunday – Daybreak

It is very early on a peaceful Sunday morning on the shoreline of the Embankment. The sky is grey and the air is cool and breezy and when the wind blows across the water which it seems to do often it is quite chilly.

Though still yawning Roger and Brian are at least awake and wrapped up from the cool morning air as they stand by the water's edge waiting for Ellie to appear. Brian has the hood of his blue top over his head and his paws shoved into the pockets of his pale blue jeans. Roger has his baggy red sweatshirt on and like Brian his paws are buried deep into the pockets of his pale brown corduroy trousers for extra warmth. As normal Roger and Brian's feet are bare so they wander around stamping their hairy little feet trying to warm them up a little bit.

'Ooh my back aches.'

Brian groans rubbing his back but Roger says nothing in return. Instead he stares out over the river Thames.

'I miss my own bed,' Brian adds.

'Yeah, well we'll be able to go home soon, hopefully,' replies Roger.

He does not look round instead he is still staring at the gently rippling water of the river Thames.

The two friends are standing on the narrow strip of beach that is little more than dirty stones and gravel. This separates the river from the man-made embankment or at least it does when the tide is out like it is now which is why they are able to stand waiting here cold and tired.

On this narrow stony beach are bits of tatty old rope and a wet brown piece of driftwood which has been washed up.

On the water of the River Thames even at this early hour a small boat chugs by, easily coping with the outgoing tide, this they both watch until the little boat passes from view.

Between glancing often to see if Ellie is arriving Roger and Brian look around at the many rather grand buildings that stand proudly along the River Thames, here at the Embankment in London. To their right almost over their heads is a railway bridge, the occasional rumble of trains passing above startles the two friends but soon they are getting used to trains running over a busy bridge.

Behind them is a large building with huge arches.

'That's Charing Cross station,' explains Roger.

'Really? I thought it was a power station,' Brian replies.

'With trains coming in and out?' questions Roger.

'Well they could be delivering coal,' Brian responds, he now feels foolish but to him this modern building does look like a power station.

There are many buildings along this stretch of the river and though they look different in size, shapes and styles they all look big and important. Besides making the river view pretty Roger and Brian look at all these buildings on both sides of the river and wonder why they were all built. But pretty scenery so early on a peaceful Sunday morning before most people have climbed out of their beds does not stop the two friends feeling cold.

'Grey,' says Brian.

He looks up at the cloudy sky, the River Thames the stone buildings and just about everything at this hour appears greyish.

'And cold.'

Roger feels the wind whip across the water almost cutting him in half. Unlike Brian he is not a hooded rat, a hat or a coat would be very useful he thinks.

'No, I mean the buildings are grey.' explains Brian.

'Oh I see. Yeah, lots of stone.' Roger responds.

'But yeah, it is a grey, cold morning.' agrees Brian.

Together the two friends stare around at the bend in the river, they see the bridges spanning the river and they watch red double-decker buses crossing from one side to the other. With the interest of good tourists they look at the many buildings further down and wonder what they are called.

Waiting for Ellie, Roger and Brian have some spare time and they know they might never see London again, so they take the opportunity to enjoy the sights.

Opposite on the South Bank they can see a building called County Hall and in front of it is the London Eye, a great big white wheel for people to ride and enjoy the views from. Already this is gently turning and even they can see this on the other side of the river. On their side of the river they can see a very fancy looking place called the Houses of Parliament which also has a famous clock with a huge bell known as Big Ben. There are many grand buildings on either side of the river and there is much to look at and admire.

All these buildings have various different reasons for being here, there are offices, railway stations, theatres for entertaining and even a hospital. But whatever their purpose to Roger and Brian they seem so proud, strong and permanent as though they have been here forever.

Roger and Brian stare in awe at the scenery, that is until they begin wondering when Ellie is going to arrive.

'Come on,' says Brian, impatiently.

From where they are standing on the narrow strip of gravel beach Roger looks beyond the washed up piece of driftwood and sees a familiar figure approaching in the distance. He soon realizes it is Ellie.

'Here she is!' he declares.

'At last!' responds Brian, he is now bored of waiting.

Smiling Ellie reaches Roger and Brian on the beach close to the water's edge. Unlike the night before the shiny blue figure hugging dress is replaced by long blue jeans dragging along the ground and almost covering her hairy bare feet. Above this she wears a long beige raincoat which restricts her long pink tail from moving too much. The glamour of the night before has gone but Ellie is still a pretty young female rat.

'Are you ready to see Nelson's Column?' asks Ellie.

'You do know where it is?' asks Roger.

'And where's your lovely shiny blue dress?' asks Brian.

Neither Ellie nor Roger bother to answer Brian's question, instead they just look at him in silence.

'Silly question?' asks Brian.

'Yes,' answers Roger.

'Oh well,' Brian replies.

Ellie does not wish for Brian to stand around feeling foolish, she realizes that he probably just misses the glitz and the glamour of the night before. Ellie knows how her fans and other rats are so impressed or even overwhelmed when they meet a star from a show. Understanding this and to spare Brian's feelings she quickly changes the subject.

'Well,' she begins, 'are you both ready?'

'Yes!' they both reply.

'Good! Let's go,' Ellie says, turning to lead them the way.

'Where are we going?' asks Brian.

Ellie stops and turns to look first at Brian and then at Roger before answering.

'Why, Trafalgar Square of course!'

'Oh of course,' mutters Brian.

Nelson's Column

Roger, Brian and Ellie stand dead still, not moving even the slightest bit. Instead they just stare upwards at the statue mounted high up on top of the great tall column that reaches many metres into the sky. Perched on top stands a proud, confident looking statue of Admiral Lord Nelson who appears to be observing his surroundings just like the real man must have done on board ship in his lifetime.

This being a statue and so high up it has the odd pigeon using his hat as a perch and the great man's shoulders are peppered with bird's mess.

At ground level but surrounding Nelson's Column on a plinth or small stage which here are made of stone are four lions, one at each corner on their own plinth as though guarding the great column. But it need not fear being taken by Roger or Brian as they stand staring upwards almost beyond their view at the statue on top.

The two friends cannot believe their eyes, they can hear the splashing and gurgling of water in the two fountains that are also part of Trafalgar Square and the sound of running water soothes them. Living in a storm drain running water is something they are used to but it is not helping them with this problem standing tall in front of them.

'So, this is it?' asks Roger.

'Yes,' answers Ellie.

'Nelson's Column?' asks Brian.

'Yes,' confirms Ellie.

'The statue the Chair-rat of the Rats Underground Southwest Drains Region wants to display on the R.U?' asks Brian.

'Um… Yes,' agrees Roger.

There is a long pause, the silence is only broken by the sound of tinkling water in the two fountains and the busy traffic which is going around Trafalgar Square. Now being later there are people out and about already, walking, chatting and feeding the many pigeons.

Still the two friends and Ellie stare up at the statue standing on top of the column which is wanted for the R.U. by Jeremy Brown, their Chair-rat and one thought strikes Roger;

'It won't fit.'

'We won't get it on the train either,' notes Brian.

Considering that Nelson's Column stands far taller than a house this is a fair observation, no person could move it so two rats have no chance.

'He won't like it.'

Roger knows that the Chair-rat expects them to deliver the statue but he also knows the Chair-rat does not really know what it looks like.

'He'll expect something,' he adds.

'So, what are we going to do?' asks Brian.

'Um…' Roger does not know what to suggest.

'Wait! I have an idea,' announces Ellie.

A little while later Roger and Brian are sitting in a boat similar to their own, but larger. They sit facing Ellie while another rat gently rows. They are below ground and would be in complete darkness if it was not for the stubs of candles on the back lighting their way and for two rats who live and work on the R.U. in the West Country this is a pleasant novelty.

'I bet you never thought you'd ever see the Rats Underground London and City Drains,' says Ellie.

'No,' they both answer, looking around.

With fascination they just sit staring at the tunnels, they have always been proud of their own R.U. network back home but this is altogether much grander.

The tunnels are larger and being so old they are lined with bricks which gives them such a pleasing appearance and of course being in London these tunnels are far more busy. In some places the R.U. here is crowded with rats and there are so many in such a hurry running along the dry banks that they even climb over each other to get to where they are going.

But the thing that makes this R.U. network so different, special even, is that unlike their own R.U. back home here the busy main routes are lit by stubs of candles. They glow dimly along one bank and though they do not give out much light it is just enough to see from one candle to the next, they do not even need the candle on their boat lit.

'Where are we going?' asks Brian.

'You'll see,' replies Ellie, mysteriously.

'Do you have a plan?' Roger asks.

'Yes, a solution, of sorts. I think your Chair-rat will like it,' she answers.

With Ellie's confidence and nothing else to do until they arrive wherever they are going the two friends sit back and enjoy the boat ride. For them it is a rare opportunity to look at the scenery and experience the R.U. of the London and City Drains region, which is such a contrast to home.

The Gift Shop

In a quiet little back street somewhere in Covent Garden sits an old almost forgotten ornament shop. It is a little shop that unfortunately is easily missed by everyone walking past. Not only does this shop sell ornaments but at the back of the shop they make them as well.

At the back of the shop is a cold, almost empty room with white-washed brick walls. In one wall beside the back door is a small window with bars giving the place an appearance of a prison cell, only the open back door letting in a draught alters this image. Along the other walls are freshly made ornaments stacked on shelves and there are plenty more sealed in boxes on the cold hard red tiled floor. Near the middle of the floor is a large wooden work bench and sitting at it on a wooden stool is an old man in a grubby shirt and blue dungarees. Working by the dim light that glows from the bare light bulb hanging from the ceiling he quietly makes more ornaments.

'Horace! Where's the chisel?' calls a voice from the front of the shop.

The voice as Horace knows belongs to Mr Smethwick, his boss.

'It's back in the toolbox Mr Smethwick sir!' Horace answers, politely, adding, 'Daft old fool,' under his breath.

Horace is barely distracted from his work by Mr Smethwick's question, he is still busy making ornaments. So busy is Horace that he does not notice the grate being carefully lifted off the small drain in the red tiled floor.

Before stepping out of the drain and onto the cold red tiled floor Roger and Brian being lead by Ellie make sure it is safe. Instantly they see Horace sitting at his workbench, they are to the right of this old man and slightly behind putting them beyond his view, unless he turns around.

'It should be safe' Ellie whispers.

'Should be?' questions Brian, very quietly.

'If we're quiet,' Ellie answers.

'Quick, and careful,' suggests Roger.

'And lucky,' adds Brian.

From the safety of the drain all three look around the room, they see the boxes on the cold red tiled floor and more importantly they see the white-washed walls with shelves stacked. They are loaded up with many different statues.

'That's where we need to go,' points Roger.

'Careful,' warns Ellie.

All three stop moving and stay dead still looking at Horace to see if he is disturbed, fortunately he carries on with his work.

Roger, Brian and Ellie know they have to be brave and quick, and they also know they will have to be a little bit lucky. It is not going to be easy.

'Oh well, let's get on with it then,' suggests Brian.

Biting back their fear all three leave the safety of the drain in the floor and sneak quickly and quietly across the floor towards the shelves. They soon reach the shelves where they see many different plain white statues and there are a few for them to choose from. On the shelves they see statues of Big Ben, Eros which the two friends instantly recognise from Piccadilly Circus and they see Tower Bridge. For some reason they see statues of a light house and they see statues of Buddha, which is a large happy fat oriental man.

'Funny, never seen him in London,' says Ellie.

'Who is it?' asks Roger.

'It's Buddha,' answers Brian.

Roger and Ellie look round at Brian in surprise, neither realized that he knows such things.

'He's a religious man from China,' Brian adds.

'Very good Brian,' praises Roger.

'But what's he doing here then?' asks Ellie.

'No idea,' admits Brian.

They hear a grunt from behind and suddenly they remember Horace is working at his bench behind them, they fall silent briefly then return to their search through the statues. Now they find something that looks familiar.

'Hey, look, is this it?' whispers Brian.

'Yeah, that's it, surely,' says Roger, uncertain, 'Is it?' he asks.

'Yes. We've found it,' agrees Ellie.

'Great. We now have an ornament of Nelson's Column,' Roger declares, quietly.

They are in fear of being seen and then caught by the old man working at his bench and now they have their statue it is definitely time for them to leave. It does not take long for Roger, Brian and Ellie to quickly agree to head back to the open drain and safety.

Brian clutches the head end of the statue while Roger struggles with the heavy base and Ellie leads them back to the drain urging them to be quick. But when you are a little rat even an ornament like this is heavy and awkward, so getting back to the drain is slow and very tiring. It is a wonder neither one drops their end but they are both puffing and panting with the strain.

Brian is carrying the head end of the statue which is thinner and a little bit lighter than the base end where Roger is struggling. But having the easier end helps Brian and he soon has a spurt of energy causing Roger to strain even more.

'Hold on, hold on!' calls Roger, urgently.

But it is too late, he drops his end of the ornament onto the hard red floor which clanks loudly. All three rats freeze in terror. Each is ready and even tempted to leave the statue of Nelson and run for safety down into the drain, but somehow they all manage to keep their nerve. Instead they stand dead still breathing quietly and staring at the old man working at his bench. But their nerve is nearly broken when Horace stops working and looks up, he does not turn around though and after a few long, painful seconds he returns to his work.

'Phew… That's a relief, that was close,' mutters Brian.

'Too close,' adds Roger.

'Never mind, anyway let's go,' Ellie orders.

'And don't rush me this time, I nearly fell over,' complains Roger.

'Sorry,' says Brian.

'You've got the easy end, the head,' Roger adds.

'Yeah, it gave me a head start,' Brian jokes.

'Right definitely, let's go!' says Ellie.

They carry the heavy and awkward statue and with Ellie's guidance they lift, twist and turn it till they are able to lower it down into the drain. But it is very hard work and their first attempt causes much shouting and complaining from all three. This suddenly ends in the statue being dropped once more only this time causing a louder noise than before.

'Quiet!' Ellie hisses.

The two friends realize she is both angry and scared, they are frightened also and realize they need to be more careful if they are to escape with the ornament of Nelson's Column.

As ordered by Ellie, Roger and Brian fall silent and again stand dead still as they watch the large old man at his workbench wondering how he will react to their noise. Horace looks up from his workbench and stares briefly at the wall in front of him for a moment, then he stoops down and has a good look under his workbench. But fortunately he does not look towards the open drain where Roger, Brian and Ellie are standing awkwardly with their little statue.

'Mr Smethwick! I think we've got mice,' Horace calls.

'Mice? He calls us mice!' complains Brian.

'They just cannot tell the difference,' moans Roger.

'Never mind that! Let's get this statue down the drain,' Ellie reminds them.

Despite feeling offended by Horace, the large old man at his bench calling them mice they are all terrified of being caught by him. With this in mind they work quickly and desperately but unlike before they work quietly trying to get the little statue down the drain.

Even though they are busy Brian finds himself thinking of the events that have brought them here and he thinks about Jeremy Brown the Chair-rat of the Rats Underground Southwest Drains Region. This causes him to think out loud;

'I hope he is grateful for this.'

'Me too!' agrees Roger.

Grunting and straining the two friends wriggle the statue around until finally they manage to get the ornament into the drain.

'I never thought we'd ever get it down here,' grunts Roger, out of breath.

'No, me neither, it's tiring,' groans Brian, also quite breathless.

They do not bother to replace the cover to the drain, instead they just haul the ornament through the small dark pipe following Ellie who like them is in a hurry to be away from there.

Several minutes later when the two friends with Ellie have long since escaped with their much prized ornament of Nelson's Column, Horace gets up from his workbench. He steps forward and trips up over the drain cover which was left lying on the floor when the three rats escaped.

'Oops! Hello, what's happened here then?' wonders Horace.

He bends down to have a look at the open drain and stares in fascination.

'How's that come loose I wonder?' he mutters.

He takes a look around and down at the open drain before replacing the cover and making sure it fits neatly and then stands up.

'Mr Smethwick! I'm putting the kettle on, do you want a cup of tea?' calls Horace.

Roger, Brian and Ellie reach the boat on the R.U. and it is only now that they begin to relax. Partly because now they are far from the gift shop they are completely safe from either harm or capture, but also because carrying the ornament has been for Roger and Brian very hard work and now they just sprawl around in the boat grunting, groaning and panting for breath.

'I'm finished,' groans Brian.

He is lying on his back with his arms and legs everywhere in an awkward mess on the floor of the boat.

'I'm totally drained,' moans Roger.

Roger is slumped against the ornament lying along the length of the boat. This boat is slightly larger than their own boat moored up back home which is just as well as there are four rats in this boat. Roger, Brian, Ellie and the rat who has been sitting patiently waiting for them to return. At least neither Roger or Brian have to row, they can lie down and rest, for now at least.

'I never want to lift that again,' Brian grumbles.

'Me neither,' agrees Roger.

'Pity,' says Ellie, 'you've got to carry it all the way home.'

'Oh yeah, nice,' groans Roger.

'Great,' says Brian thinking it is anything but great.

'Shame we can't post it,' suggests Roger.

'No, but you can do the next best thing,' Ellie replies.

'Which is?' asks Brian, sitting up hopefully.

'You can go by rail. You get to have a rest on a nice overnight train journey,' answers Ellie.

'Oh good, I can't wait...'

Brian responds, not feeling at all happy. He lies down in the boat again and closes his eyes resting. He knows there is no way of escaping the hard work he and Roger have to face until they have delivered the ornament of Nelson's Column.

'I thought you had a nice little solution for us then,' says Roger, feeling disappointed.

London and City Drains – Again

After several minutes resting Roger and Brian have recovered enough to sit up in the boat. They see the rower in his brown tweed trousers and jacket and dark brown baseball cap slowly rowing the now heavy boat.

It makes a change for Brian and especially Roger to sit back, relax and simply be passengers on the R.U. and they do not wish to miss the chance to enjoy the scenery.

The London and City Drains Region is still such a novelty to them with its many brick-lined tunnels which for the two friends create the ideal image of a sewer network. And yet a brick-lined tunnel is not common back home, there most tunnels of the R.U. are large concrete tubes. But the things that make this a special Rats Underground are the tea lights which line the main routes giving enough light for rats down here to see where they are going. The two friends normally rely on the small stub of candle most boats have stuck on the bow right at the front, that and the occasional shaft of light coming through the storm drains. Otherwise they are used to travelling in darkness depending on their ability to see well in the dark which for creatures that are often active during the night is very useful.

Also the London and City R.U. is much busier than what Roger and Brian are used to back home. With many boats going up and down the dirty stream of water and many rats walking along the banks the place is busy and even noisy. Plus there are many turnings branching off the main routes with even more traffic.

But what grabs the two friends' interest are the crowds of rats wandering back and forth, singly, in two's and even in noisy groups chatting while they move busily to wherever they are heading. The banks of the London and City R.U., Ellie assures them, are often crowded and busy for many hours of the day and night.

Being in London and travelling on their R.U. is exciting and Roger and Brian sit back, relax and enjoy the great buzzing atmosphere of the Capital both above and below ground. They like being home but they also enjoy travel because it is a chance to try something different, an opportunity to see and do things you normally can only think about. And now down here in London they have briefly even forgotten about the quest their Chair-rat has sent them on even though the statue is in the boat beside them. So naturally they are not considering that if it was not for their quest they would not have done all the things they have been enjoying this weekend.

But instead they just relax and feel happy as they look around themselves and commit to memory the sights and sounds of London.

'I'm hungry,' says Brian, all of a sudden.

Roger looks round at his friend near him in the boat as they float gently hearing the gentle creak and splash of the oars. For a moment he just stares saying nothing.

'So am I!' Roger admits, finally.

'Don't worry, I've thought about that,' reassures Ellie.

'Oh good,' says Brian.

'Really?' asks Roger.

'Of course, we need to eat sometime,' replies Ellie. Feeling hungry and knowing they are heading towards a meal the two friends sit up and watch eagerly wondering where they are going. Now the boat turns up a quieter stretch of the R.U. here it is no longer lit by tea lights but they can still see by the small stub of candle on the bow of their boat. In front they see a very smelly swirling mist hanging over the murky water. It is almost enough to ruin their appetites. But only almost.

'Phew! Whiffy,' complains Roger.

'Yuk! Let's get out of here. So we can breathe, and then eat,' suggests Brian, quite wisely.

Their stomachs are rumbling now as they follow Ellie on foot upwards towards the surface. On Ellie's instruction and promise of its safety they leave the ornament of Nelson's Column lying in the boat. The rat in a brown tweed jacket and trousers who rowed them there will be keeping it in the boat. Then he will go and deliver it to Paddington Station for the next part of their journey.

'So it is quite safe,' Ellie assures them.

Meanwhile the two hungry friends follow Ellie to wherever she is leading them for something to eat, though where they do not know, Ellie is keeping it a surprise.

All three have been walking along narrow pipes for a while, but now at last they can see a small shaft of daylight ahead. A short distance to go and they will discover where Ellie is leading them and more importantly the two friends will be able to feed their empty rumbling stomachs.

'Are we nearly there yet?' asks a hungry Brian.

The shaft of daylight in front instead of reassuring Brian has made him feel impatient, especially as his guts are beginning to growl quite loudly.

'Nearly,' answers Ellie.

'How nearly?' pursues Brian.

'Oh, very nearly,' assures Ellie.

No sooner than Ellie has finished saying her words of comfort to Brian than they step from the darkness of the tunnel into bright clear daylight. Now they can see where Ellie has brought them and the first thing they notice is a great stone monument with an archway. This is really big, it is easily big enough for people to stroll through if it did not have gates securely locked, but being so big it towers over the three hungry rats. On either side are smaller open arches but even these are big enough for people to go through and the whole thing looks like a huge porch or gateway. The stone monument also has columns and pictures carved into the stonework but none of this is colourful though, instead it is all a plain light grey, almost white in colour. 'Welcome to Marble Arch!' greets Ellie.

'I've heard of this place,' admits Brian.

'You have, have you?' asks Roger, surprised.

'No need to sound so surprised. I've heard of some things.'

Brian is a little upset, his friend seems a bit too surprised that he should know such things.

'Oh sorry,' says Roger.

Being rats and therefore only little, Marble Arch appears to them as a massive entrance.

'Where does it lead?' asks Brian.

'Nowhere,' answers Ellie.

'Really?' questions Roger.

He looks around at the monument and where it is placed for several moments, he cannot help but wonder;

'What's it doing here then?'

'Um… I don't know, it's just a famous landmark, people come here all the time.'

Ellie answers as best she can, but even though the question is simple she does not know the answer.

'Yes, there are a lot of people around,' Brian observes.

'But you're right, I heard once that it was a gateway,' Ellie explains.

'You mean like a fancy porch?' asks Brian.

'Yes, I suppose.'

All three just look around at the traffic which they see moving in every direction they look, they are surrounded by roads but none lead to where they are standing and nothing leads from the arches.

'It's not any use now though,' Roger observes, sharply.

'Anyway never mind that, we're here to eat!' Ellie changes the subject.

'Food!' Brian exclaims happily.

They sit safely hidden beneath a park bench beside the monument of Marble Arch where they hungrily tuck into their lunches. For Roger, Brian and Ellie lunch comes out of a flimsy red box thrown down lazily by some person who must have had enough themselves. Left behind, for them inside the flimsy red box are some now cold chips with remnants of bread and salad plus a few other bits and pieces. These are all just scraps but the three hungry rats do not mind, it is enough to keep them going for a few hours at least.

From beneath the wooden park bench that serves as their own personal restaurant they enjoy the surprisingly good view around them. Of course close up their view mostly is of the legs of people wandering around the famous monument. These they know are tourists seeing the sights and some are even taking pictures.

But it is when they look further away they see an interesting view of a busy London and its famous streets. Behind the park bench they can see Park Lane, this has a dual carriageway which is two roads running side by side with a lot of traffic going either way. Looking down Park Lane on the left they can just about see some very grand buildings lining the big road, a lot of these are shops and posh hotels which do not appeal much to Roger and Brian. Opposite on the right of Park Lane is Hyde Park, this does appeal to the two friends as it is a big wide open space, they do like being where it is green and peaceful.

'Hey Rog, that looks familiar,' says Brian, pointing.

'Yeah, that's where we went yesterday morning,' answers Roger.

'Is it? Oh yeah,' Brian slowly realizes.

They can see quite a few people wandering around at the entrance of Hyde Park Corner. All three know that even people need to escape from the noise and the chaos of their busy lives and a little bit of greenery helps to calm them down just as well as it does for the two friends.

'I bet it's quieter over there than it is here,' suggests Brian.

Under their park bench they are still very near to people wandering around which makes them feel a need to hide further under their bench. They are close to Oxford Street and its many shops and though this is a traffic island surrounded by busy roads there are crossings and subways helping everyone reach this monument.

'Yeah, but food is here,' Ellie replies.

'Yum.' Roger is busy stuffing cold chips into his hungry face.

But now between oversized mouthfuls of food Roger's interest is drawn in another direction. Now he is looking straight ahead.

Little Cairo

A big red double-decker bus all lit up and glowing goes past and up another road and seeing the bus glowing so well he realizes it is getting dark which means it is getting late already. It has been a busy and so far quick day for Roger and Brian.

'I didn't know it was that late,' admits Roger.

'That explains why we're so hungry,' adds Brian.

'Yes, it is not easy getting a statue of Nelson's Column, takes careful planning,' Ellie says.

'We have been busy again, today.'

Roger observes, but his attention is still drawn by the red double-decker bus which has pulled up neatly at a bus stop.

'Ellie?' begins Roger.

'Yes?'

'What's up there?'

Roger asks while he stretches out his arm and points with his paw up the road and almost strikes a pigeon.

'Get out of the way,' says Roger, to the pigeon.

'Coo,' says the pigeon.

'Can anyone speak pigeon?' asks Roger.

'Not a word,' answers Ellie.

'Oh well, anyway, what's up there?'

He returns to his question and again Roger points with his paw but this time the pigeon, along with the others, keeps a safer distance. These pigeons are busily cooing among themselves, Roger suspects they are complaining about them, especially for not sharing the junk food from the flimsy red box. Clearly this does not bother them as they keep on eating hungrily. Brian shoves yet another long cold chip into his wide open mouth while Ellie nibbles on a piece of bread coated in sesame seeds. This piece of bread has a tatty bit of now floppy green lettuce glued to it by mayonnaise, adding flavour. Roger however is shovelling bits of everything into his hungry mouth with both paws.

'Up there? That's Edgware Road, known as Little Cairo.' Ellie replies.

'Little Cairo?' Brian responds, surprised.

'Yes, I'll show you it later, on the bus,' answers Ellie.

'Why Little Cairo?' Roger asks Ellie, barely between mouthfuls and even during mouthfuls of chips and bread, not a pretty sight…

'Well, you'll see. All I will say is that it has a wonderful Arab flavour to the place,' explains Ellie, with some mystery.

Shortly the two friends are filled with curiosity for Edgware Road and all three are filled completely with gone cold junk food and once again the flimsy red box is thrown aside.

Now Ellie leads them away heading towards a bus stop as they prepare to catch a bus to take them down Edgware Road to see Little Cairo. Within a few minutes a big red double-decker bus appears, on the front above the driver in white letters on a black background it says "Edgware Road" and "Paddington Station".

'Ah, this is the one!' Ellie declares, adding, 'Get ready to board.'

The big red bus comes alongside and stopping briefly in traffic all three quietly and quickly leap aboard and just in time. Roger, Brian and Ellie hold on tight to the pole at the doorway as the bus begins moving away again quickly. From this step on the bus they have a nice view of the street as they pass along.

RESTAURANT 0207

Roger and Brian pay attention and try enjoying the scenery and doing their best they manage to see a long busy street with big tall buildings which line both sides of the road. They do notice the place has an Arabic appearance which is how it gets its nickname of Little Cairo. Shop fronts have Arab writing on their signs which to them is wriggly and unreadable. The restaurants here serve Arab food while outside they can see men in white long flowing Arab clothing sitting while smoking hookahs. This is like a huge bottle with some fruity, spicy liquid inside and it has a tube attached with a pipe on the end.

Roger and Brian see all these things and more, besides which they enjoy so much but the bus is moving so fast they are being blown by the wind which makes their eyes water. Through the blurry vision of watery eyes they view this interesting road but soon they are overcome by the effects of speed. Feeling the wind blowing through their fur they simply face the wind and enjoy the fun of speed.

'Wee!' yells Brian, playfully.

Rats, Roger and Brian included, do not tend to ride on buses, other forms of transport yes, occasionally but not buses. Though not the first bus ride this weekend this is still a novelty and now they have managed to find a statue for their Chair-rat they can relax and enjoy themselves. Unfortunately Roger unwisely stops holding onto the pole. The bus suddenly brakes, grinding noisily to a halt, but Roger is hurled forward running headlong into the metal wall of the bus sending used tickets flying. Brian and Ellie burst out laughing at the sight of Roger's misfortune. Staggering he makes his way back to the pole and this time makes sure he keeps holding on tightly.

'You ok?' asks Brian, kindly, though only after he has stopped laughing.

Roger does not answer, instead he stands panting for breath feeling winded from his collision.

The bus soon gets going again and this time all three hold on very tight to the pole, neither of them wish to get hurt and after Roger's funny accident they realize they need to be more careful. Now the bus moves slower and they all spend the rest of the journey enjoying what is left of the scenery. Soon the bus turns into another road and Ellie senses they are close to their destination and she warns the two friends to be ready to leave the bus. Fortunately a person rings the bell and at the next stop the bus grinds safely to a halt.

'Here we are!' announces Ellie.

The bus grinds to a halt at the bus stop and people step off into the street and walk away. Roger, Brian and Ellie seeing all is safe and clear soon follow the other passengers as they climb down quietly and carefully onto the path. Now they patiently stand by the kerb facing the big red double-decker bus.

'Well, where is the train station from here then?' asks Brian.

The double-decker bus pulls away from the bus stop and now across the road in front of them they can see Paddington train station.

'Ah… There it is,' he mutters quietly.

'Look over there Brian, it looks like a wedding cake,' points Roger.

To their left is a very grand, pretty white building with large windows and "GWR" in stone, high up on the front of this is part of the train station. But like all the other passengers what they are interested in is the entrance that will lead them to the trains and more importantly their train. In their case the freight train to the west. For a moment all three stand on the kerb staring into the darkness of the gloomy entrance that will lead them into the train station. The entrance into Paddington station is up a short lane but first they must cross the road.

'Almost time to catch our train home Brian,' says Roger.

'Yeah, soon be home and back on the R.U. our R.U. that is,' adds Brian.

'And your Chair-rat will get his statue of Nelson's Column,' Ellie reminds them.

'Oh yeah, he will,' agrees Brian.

Homeward Bound

Since beginning their adventure Roger and Brian have been in a hurry. They have been trying desperately to get the job done so they could return home and back to their peaceful life. The two friends have both been eager to go home, relax in their storm drain and wander safely and happily around the Rats Underground. But now they have nearly completed their quest for the column they no longer wish it to end. They have been so busy in their quest that neither Roger or Brian realized how much fun they were having. Since arriving in London they have found more than just the column with Nelson on top. They have seen some famous sights in London allowing them to feel like tourists on holiday, also, and more interesting for them, they have discovered the Rats Underground. The London and City Drains Region and this, they both feel is much better than their own very familiar one back home.

Adding to the feeling of being on holiday Roger and Brian have sampled some great nightlife, firstly with seeing London all lit up and busy and secondly enjoying some wonderful music. Finding a nightclub where rats could relax, enjoy themselves and hear good music is something the two friends will always remember.

But more important than all this Roger and Brian have gained a good new friend in the shape of Ellie. She has been so kind and helpful to them and without her help they might never have found Nelson's Column. And if they did they might not have found a nice small statue easy enough to carry home so the Chair-rat could display it on the Rats Underground later.

After crossing the road all three are quickly under one of the big arches of the huge roof that covers Paddington station. Ignored or simply not noticed by the many people in the train station Ellie quickly leads them down and along one of the platforms. After a very long walk they go down a concrete slope and begin walking among the rail tracks. Here it is very dangerous for people as they can get hit by a fast-moving train, so here being rats they feel quite safe and they already feel relaxed. Looking up, in the distance they can see the freight train waiting silently and alone on the rails.

'Is that our train?' asks Brian.

'Yes, that's it, shan't be leaving for a while yet though,' answers Ellie.

'Are you sure?' asks Roger.

'Yes, the ones we use only leave after dark,' Ellie replies.

'But it is dark,' notes Brian, looking up at the black sky.

'Yes, well, it is still too early for that to be leaving,' Ellie assures them.

'Ok,' says Brian.

'They leave in darkness and arrive in daylight,' Ellie adds.

'So really our freight train is a night train,' says Roger.

'The ones we use usually are, it's safer in darkness, less people around and those that are don't usually care if they see a rat,' explains Ellie.

'It's much the same back home,' Roger adds.

They step carefully over the gravel which surrounds the railway tracks, now Roger and Brian are walking behind Ellie as they walk alongside the freight train which will take them home.

This freight train, like most freight trains which carry goods, is very long and with a variety of different carriages.

There are big metal skips which can carry coal, gravel, sand or anything loose that can be piled up high, also there are a few long cylinder-shaped carriages which can hold liquid or even gas. But, as before, the two friends are heading towards a wooden wagon, a rather grubby wooden box car with a sliding door which is often used for moving farm animals. This will be their transport home which fortunately they do not have to share with any farm animals tonight.

It is night time, the sun set long ago and the sky is black but this part of the railway track is lit up very well by bright spotlights pointing downwards. In this bright light Roger and Brian see a rat in green R.U. overalls similar to the ones they wear when working back home.

When doing their grubby but necessary work of clearing dirt and mess out of the R.U. Roger and Brian wear a green one piece boiler suit and a green baseball cap. On the breast pocket and on the baseball cap is the Rats Underground logo which is a yellow R above and to the left of a yellow U inside a blue circle. The London and City Drains Region uniform is almost the same except for the logo. Their logo is a blue circle with a red bar running left to right with the letters L&C RU in bold white within the red bar.

But they are not really looking at the rat in the green overalls, nor are they paying much attention to the different logo, instead they are looking at what this rat is standing beside. He is standing patiently holding onto the little ornament of Nelson's Column.

'That's our statue Rog!' declares Brian, almost excitedly.

'Yeah, we've got to get that thing home yet,' replies Roger.

'Oh yeah, it's heavy and awkward and we'll have to carry it again,' remembers Brian.

The two friends feel they must have blinked or something because the next moment to their amazement they notice the rat in the green overalls has suddenly disappeared. Despite being lit up so brightly he has somehow vanished into the darkness beyond and now their statue stands completely alone.

'Where's he gone?' asks Roger.

'You saw him too? I was beginning to think I was seeing things… Where's he gone then?' replies Brian.

'Oh that's ok, he's got work to do,' Ellie explains.

'What, at night?' asks Roger.

'Yes, London is a big busy place and it's busy all day and all through the Night,' answers Ellie.

Still following Ellie, Roger and Brian reach their statue which is standing below the open sliding door of the box car they will soon be boarding. It is time to say goodbye. For almost a minute all three just stand silently feeling awkward not knowing what to say.

'Oh well… Time we went,' sighs Roger.

'Yes,' agrees Ellie.

'Back home again,' adds Brian, trying to be cheerful.

'Yes,' repeats Ellie.

'Time to say goodbye, eh Brian?' says Roger, also trying to be cheerful.

'It is, unless… Well,' Brian begins.

'Yes, as Brian says, unless… Um,' agrees Roger, vaguely.

An embarrassed silence falls between all three of them as neither one quite knows what to say next. But Roger and Brian clearly wish to share an idea they have.

'Well, we've got a nice place,' Roger blurts out.

'Yeah! We have. Right on the Rats Underground. Southwest Drains Region of course,' adds Brian, quickly.

'Of course,' agrees Ellie.

'It's really quite nice, our home,' assures Roger.

'It's great!' adds Brian, with enthusiasm.

'Close to the town and next to the football ground,' Roger boasts.

'A great atmosphere really, you'd like it,' suggests Brian.

Slowly their confidence is growing even though the two friends are still waffling rather than just saying what they are thinking.

'Yes!' says Roger and feeling positive he adds, 'that's an idea! Why don't you come and join us? You're more than welcome.'

'Thank you Roger and Brian, but...' Ellie begins.

Already beginning to feel quite disheartened Roger and Brian can only listen to Ellie and hope she can be persuaded to join them both.

'You see... Well it is very nice of you both to invite me but...' Ellie stops again.

'But?' asks Roger.

'There's plenty of room,' Brian says, full of hope.

'No, you see London is my home. This is where I belong, where I can sing in my band, the Blue J's,' Ellie explains, finally.

Poor Roger and Brian, the two friends shoulders drop with a sense of disappointment, with Ellie's kind help and good company they have both enjoyed themselves so much. Yet they realize what Ellie says is true, she does belong here in London, with her band, even though they cannot help feeling a little bit upset.

'Sorry,' says Ellie, kindly.

An unhappy silence falls between them as Roger and Brian still wish Ellie would join them and even though they have had so much fun Ellie knows they must return home with their statue.

'I tell you what,' suggests Ellie, 'if we swap addresses we can visit each other!'

'Yeah ok!' agrees Roger.

'Good idea!' adds Brian.

It is an idea that brightens everyone's mood and they all wish to end on a high note.

Suddenly from the darkness beyond the floodlights they hear something which makes them all feel quite nervous...

Somewhere in this dark night where the floodlights do not glow they can hear the sound of gravel crunching underfoot and it is so loud and heavy they know it is not the sound of another rat approaching. Peering through the gloom into the dark shadows along the track they see a figure approaching. It is the figure of a man in dirty orange overalls carrying a lunch box in one hand and a bag in the other. The man is heading in their direction as he goes towards the engine far up at the front.

'Quick, hide!' declares Roger, quickly.

All three quickly run underneath the train and hide behind one of the metal wheels. Here they are out of sight of the man in overalls as they wait for him to pass but while waiting for the man to walk by they suddenly realize they have made a mistake.

'Hey Rog, look,' points Brian.

They all look and discover that they have left the ornament of Nelson's Column standing alone and forgotten and worse still exposed.

'It will have to stay there,' Ellie responds, coolly.

'We can't move that thing quickly anyway,' admits Roger.

With nothing else to do but wait and hope all three hide silently behind the metal wheel of the train. Here they can see and hear as the man in orange overalls gets closer to their hiding place and to their little statue. Crunch, crunch, crunch his feet go on the gravel getting steadily louder as he gets steadily closer. Crunch, crunch, crunch. The man in orange overalls is very close now and they can see him so well from where they are hiding.

'Rog, he's close,' says Brian.

'I know,' he replies.

'I hope he doesn't see our statue,' Brian says.

'Me too,' Roger agrees.

'I just hope he doesn't tread on it,' Ellie remarks.

'Ah, I hadn't thought of that,' admits Roger.

Now all three watch the man closely as he nears them and more importantly gets very close to the ornament of Nelson's Column. All three went to so much trouble in getting the statue they do not want it broken by a careless foot now and worryingly the statue is right in his path. Crunch, crunch, crunch his feet keep going on the gravel. He is almost beside their hiding place now and all three hold their breath, partly for fear of being seen but mostly for fear of losing their statue. Crunch, crunch, crunch, each step brings the man closer still and all they can do is wait and hope. Crunch, crunch, crunch and the man's footstep lands right beside the statue barely missing it but leaving it undamaged.

'Phew! That was close,' Roger sighs with relief.

'Yeah, lucky too!' adds Brian.

All three step out from behind the metal wheel and return to their statue. Ellie looks in the direction of the man in orange overalls and sees him climb into the cab of the engine at the front.

'He's the driver,' she observes.

'The driver?' repeats Roger.

'I suppose we'd better get going then,' Brian suggests.

'Yes, It's almost time to go,' agrees Roger.

'You'd better get moving, the drivers round here never hang around for very long,' Ellie advises.

As though to prove her point the driver starts up the engine and the train is soon chugging and shaking as it waits in the sidings. Feeling a sense of urgency Roger and Brian decide they must get themselves and their little statue of Nelson's Column up into the box car ready for their journey home.

'Better climb aboard, hadn't we Rog?' suggests Brian.

'Yes, we had better,' agrees Roger.

Brian quickly climbs up into the wooden box car and once he is safely on board the train he turns around and looks down at his friend.

'Ok, pass it up.'

Knowing Brian is ready Roger begins lifting the little statue of Nelson's Column which on his own means a lot of straining and struggling. With much grunting and groaning he manages to lift it up off the ground and with much more struggling he manages to lift it up to Brian. Now Brian takes the little statue of Nelson's Column and dragging it he gets it safely up on board the train. Roger is breathless from the effort but the train is ready to go and he does not wish to be left behind, so he gathers his strength and climbs up on board the train beside his friend.

'Oh well, goodbye Ellie, keep in touch,' says Roger.

'I will,' she replies.

'Good. And visit us!' calls Brian.

'I shall,' Ellie assures.

They do not spend long on their goodbyes. As Ellie had warned the driver is ready to begin their long, slow journey through the night and now the train begins moving away from the sidings.

'We're off! Bye!' yells Roger, waving.

'Bye Ellie, keep in touch!' yells Brian, also waving.

'I shall, bye! Bye Roger. Bye Brian. Goodbye!' Ellie replies, waving.

The freight train is moving away and the gap between them is quickly growing. Now they can only wave goodbye and within minutes the darkness of the night and the growing distance separate Roger and Brian from Ellie. Now the two friends sit down on the floor of the train listening to the gentle clanking, creaking and rattling as the train rolls along the track.

'Oh well...' sighs Brian.

'Yes...It was a nice trip to London,' Roger decides.

Silently the two friends sit back and look at the little statue of Nelson's Column which is beside them on the train, it is after all the reason they came to London and the reason they are now able to go home. Without the Chair-rat sending them on a quest for this statue they would probably never have met Ellie or had the fun they had in London. But they did, and now they have said goodbye and are now on their way back home.

'Well, at least we can soon sleep in our own beds again,' notes Brian.

'True, I miss my bed, it's nice, warm and cosy and just how I like it,' admits Roger.

'Unfortunately we have to sleep on the floor of this freight train tonight,' moans Brian.

'Yeah, I'll have an achy back tomorrow,' Roger complains.

The bright lights of London are soon behind them. After passing through some small towns on the outskirts of London they begin entering the countryside. It is night time and now they are in the countryside the train is in complete darkness and box cars are not lit up so the two friends can see very little. Roger and Brian sit staring out at the open sliding door but it is completely dark so they can see nothing but blackness and even they are unable to see anything.

Instead they become aware of the noises made by the freight train as it clanks, rattles and groans on its slow journey through the night. The noises of the train are slow and rhythmic, it is quite soothing and this is enough to relax Roger and Brian and make them both feel sleepy. Curling up and going to sleep is not a bad idea but now the two friends realize other rats are on this train. Some are already asleep while others have just settled down. If Roger and Brian were not feeling so tired and sleepy they would peer through the darkness and recognise some of the other passengers on their train. The two friends are unaware that they are sharing their box car with the domino players who, like them, are making a return journey. This time, however, they are too tired to play dominoes, instead they are already fast asleep. They are all huddled up together for warmth and show no signs of waking any time soon.

Following the good example set by all sleeping rats on board this train the two friends decide to snuggle up together for warmth. They make themselves as comfortable as possible on the hard wooden floor of the train and settle down for a decent night's sleep.

'Night, Rog.'

'Night, Brian.'

They listen to the creaks of the train and allow the gentle rocking to lull them quickly to sleep.

Through the still quiet darkness of night the train rolls creaking and rattling along the lonely empty track. And a patchy blanket of cloud drifts by beneath the starry moonlit sky while this freight train pulls its long heavy load ever onwards. Through dark woods and alongside rolling green hills and by fields of growing crops this train keeps going without speeding up, slowing down or stopping to rest.

Occasionally the freight train slowly passes through a town where the place is gloomily lit in a dull orange glow from the streetlights. The town like all the others it passes is calm as its people sleep soundly in their beds until morning when the peace and quiet will yet again be disturbed.

While the train rolls along the sleeping rats barely stir, just like the townsfolk they all feel safe and warm.

After their adventures Roger and Brian are happily in a deep sleep while the train does the hard work of carrying them all the way back home.

After several hours, many miles and a few towns the freight train is close to its destination and more importantly for Roger and Brian at least, getting close to their home town.

All the rats riding on the freight train are still sleeping and very few barely even stir. Slowly the sun begins rising giving the black sky a thin line of blue and orange far away on the horizon. After a while the black night sky becomes dark blue and gently, slowly, almost carefully fades lighter, while all the rats are sleeping a new day is dawning.

Monday Morning – Arrival

Hours have passed since the two friends hurriedly climbed on board this freight train and the scenery outside has now completely changed. Now there is daylight and the sky is pale grey, almost white in colour as the sky is full of cloud. But there appears little threat of rain just the promise of a cool, dull day as the cloud hangs low over the freight train while Roger and Brian are still sleeping.

After pulling its long and heavy load through the night the freight train has now completed its journey. Now it sits quietly in the sidings silent and unmoving as it has been doing for the last five minutes. And still Roger and Brian do not stir instead they just keep on sleeping and since the train has stopped moving it also stopped gently rocking but even this has not woken them up. Roger and Brian are enjoying a nice long sleep after a nice big adventure, even though really they would prefer to do this in their own beds.

After several minutes Brian slowly stirs, soon he groans and stretches, then he realises the train is no longer moving. Brian is suddenly wide awake and alarmed, he looks out of the open sliding door and sees broad daylight entering the wooden box car. Then Brian looks around the box car and notices that all the other rats that were sleeping last night have long gone, only he and Roger remain.

'Rog, Rog, wake up Roger. The train has stopped and everyone's gone, hey Rog!' calls Brian, urgently.

Roger is still blissfully sleeping and showing no sign of waking.

'Rog!' Brian tries again, 'the train's stopped, we must be back home Rog.'

Brian's urgency and persistence slowly begins to work as Roger wakes. Groaning and stretching Roger just lays still trying to return to sleep but Brian won't let him he gently rocks his friend trying to wake him and get his attention.

'Uh, what?' Roger grunts.

Despite laying on the hard wooden floor of the box car Roger is quite comfortable and wishes to finish his nice long sleep undisturbed so he does not sit up, he does not even open his eyes.

'I said we're home. Well, the train has stopped,' explains Brian.

These words however have an amazing effect on the sleepy Roger, it has the kind of effect Brian has been trying to achieve for a few minutes.

'Stopped?' asks Roger.

'Yeah.'

'Home?' asks Roger.

'Yeah, well I think so, let's have a look,' suggests Brian.

Roger is wide awake now and quickly the two friends get up and go to the open sliding door where they can see clearly and quite far. As soon as they reach the door and look out they find themselves up on a railway bridge peering down into the roads below. There they see cars parked in a quiet narrow road while noisy traffic is flowing round the corner, but on the corner they see the Kestrel Fish Bar. Now the two friends look at each other.

'We're home!' both declare, excitedly.

To keep people safe from the big, fast-moving trains the track is separated either by walls or fences and in some places, like here, the railway line is separated by a wire fence, it is the kind that forms little squares covered in thin green plastic. Also, adding privacy on the outside the fence is partly hidden by a large scruffy hedge, the kind that unfortunately has litter strewn all over the grassy ground.

Sitting down, leaning against this green coated wire fence so close to the railway tracks is a scruffy man with messy hair and lots of stubble over his face, for warmth he wears a grubby old overcoat covered in stains. This man is drinking something from a bottle wrapped in a plain brown paper bag. He sits alone hidden by the hedge enjoying his early morning drink while occasionally looking over his shoulder at the railway hoping to see trains going along or simply to pass the time. He has plenty of time and he has his bottle, he also has a nice quiet place to spend his time.

Roger and Brian have climbed down from the freight train and now they begin lugging the heavy and rather awkward little statue of Nelson's Column. With Roger at the front and Brian behind they struggle along over the gravel that covers the ground surrounding the railway tracks. For two little rats this is heavy work and they struggle and strain to carry the ornament towards the train station so they can reach their boat tied up safely on the Rats Underground.

'I think I've got the heavy end.' complains Brian.

'Really? I thought I had the heavy end,' replies Roger.

'Well I haven't got the light end!' Brian retorts.

'I don't think there is a light end,' suggests Roger.

It is not everyday that you are lucky enough to see two rats walking along chatting to each other. Nor is it likely that one will be wearing a baggy red sweatshirt and the other a hooded blue top. But to see all this while they are carrying an ornament of Nelson's Column is very unusual, not something you expect to see rats doing at all.

On seeing this unusual sight the man in the grubby old overcoat takes a long hard look at the bottle wrapped in the brown paper bag. After a moment's serious thought he throws the bottle away in a mixture of fear and disgust before getting up off the ground and hastily leaving the privacy of the hedge. The man cannot leave this place quickly enough.

'I ain't touching another drop!' he declares. On stepping out from behind the hedge the man in the grubby overcoat runs away, it is not clear where he is going but the further seems to be the better.

The once smart, clean boat-shaped fruit bowl that now serves Roger and Brian so well as their boat sits tied up securely in the murky water of the dark and damp Rats Underground. Wooden spoons, or oars as the two friends know them sit in the boat facing forward ready for use.

Roger and Brian are still carrying their ornament, but happily for them they are on the Rats Underground now and even better, for the first time in days they see their very own boat. Catching their breath they stop and rest and simply stare at their boat, a pleasant sight which instantly makes them both feel much happier.

'We're back on the R.U. Our R.U.,' says Brian, happily.

'Which means, we're home,' Roger adds.

'I'm glad really,' Brian admits.

'Me too, it's nice to be back,' agrees Roger, cheerfully.

The two friends pick up their ornament again and take the final few steps towards their boat. Struggling they carefully lower the statue of Nelson's Column into the boat taking care not to drop it into the dirty smelly water or worse still capsize the boat which would probably end up with it sinking. Once safely on board, the ornament they discover uses up a lot of space and Brian sits cramped while Roger is forced into a slightly awkward position for rowing.

They have only been away for a couple of days but Roger and Brian cannot help but look around at the familiar sight of the gloomy tunnel of the R.U. They have had such a busy adventure that both feel as though they have been away for far longer. After a moment Roger looks at his friend sitting opposite him.

'Well,' he says, 'it's Monday morning.'

'Yeah, normally we'd be at work,' Brian observes.

This is quite true. Every Monday, because Roger and Brian live on the Rats Underground they have to work to keep it in good order. Unfortunately their job is to use a pick and shovel and clear the smelly muck that sometimes causes blockages. But as yet the two friends have not yet returned from their quest that Jeremy Brown, the Chair-rat of the Rats Underground Southwest Drains Region had sent them. Until they deliver the ornament of Nelson's Column they are still on their quest.

'What would you like to do now Brian?' asks Roger.

'Go home to bed, put my feet up and relax,' answers Brian.

'Me too, really,' admits Roger.

'But?' asks Brian.

Brian likes his own idea very much, he just wants to go home and relax but he has an horrible feeling that this is not going to happen, not yet anyway. He suspects that Roger has other plans.

'But?' asks Brian, again.

'Well…' begins Roger, slowly.

'Yes?'

'I think we should get rid of this awkward, heavy thing as soon as possible,' Roger explains.

He taps his hairy bare foot moodily against the ornament of Nelson's Column and Brian senses his frustration.

'Why are you in such a hurry to get rid of it then Rog?' asks Brian.

'The sooner we deliver it the sooner we get back to normal,' answers Roger.

'And back to work,' adds Brian.

Being Monday the two friends should be working hard somewhere on the Rats Underground.

'Oh yeah, of course, I never thought of that.' admits Roger.

'The Chair-rat might expect us to work today,' suggests Brian.

'What? After all we've done? We've had the whole weekend away looking for this!'

Not for the first time Roger taps his hairy bare foot against the ornament resting in their boat.

'True,' agrees Brian. 'Ok, let's go, but slowly.' Maybe it is a good thing or perhaps it is a bad thing but Roger and Brian's journey from just outside the train station to their head office is only a short one. Hastings House, the head office of the Rats Underground Southwest Drains Region is hidden somewhere just below the bus station. For people walking above ground this is past a pub then just round the corner and across a road but for rats this journey is much more simple. There are no roads to cross and their route runs almost in a straight line until they reach a sign pointing left. Here it simply says "R U H O" in white letters written on a grey wooden plank which is cut badly but all the same it points the way.

'Oh well, here we go,' says Brian, nervously.

Roger says nothing, instead he just keeps rowing their heavily loaded boat.

It is quite late in the morning and at this time of day the Rats Underground just outside the head office is dead quiet. No traffic and no rats wandering around, all are at work or simply elsewhere.

'Everyone's keeping away,' Roger remarks.

'I don't blame them,' says Brian.

The two friends reach the closed door of Hastings House, in short they are at their head office so they climb out of their boat and step onto the dirty but dry concrete ground beside the sealed entrance. Once out of their boat they struggle to get their little statue of Nelson's Column onto the dry ground outside the door ready for delivery.

'Do you think it matters that we really have an ornament?' asks Brian.

'Shush Brian! Anyway, no, not really,' answers Roger, cautiously.

They are standing outside the stern looking round wooden door feeling nervous. They look at the slightly grubby little brass plaque saying "Southwest Drains. Chair-rat Jeremy Brown". After staring at this for a long moment the two friends turn and look at each other.

'Oh well Brian.'

'Oh well Roger.'

Still the two friends stand there, they are yet to knock on the door but they have not plucked up enough courage to see the Chair-rat who after all is a powerful and very important rat on the R.U.

'Can't we just leave it on the doorstep?' asks Brian, nodding towards the ornament.

'Yes, no! We can't do that... I wish we could, but no... Better not,' decides Roger. The two friends are still getting ready to knock on the door when suddenly Brian notices something is missing, something they considered pointless and annoying yet thought was important.

'Where's the big guard gone?' he asks, 'I thought he stood at this day all day everyday.'

'I don't know, maybe it's his day off. He was annoying anyway,' replies Roger.

When they were ordered to visit Hastings House the big guard at the door made it quite difficult for them to gain entrance, even though they did not really want to be there. A very large rat dressed much like a policeman blocking their way was, at the time, a little intimidating, only a little though they soon found the guard quite annoying. Now he appears not to be here leaving their entrance blocked only by a closed door.

Despite all this the two friends are still standing outside the closed round wooden door that separates them from the head office of the Rats Underground Southwest Drains Region. They are just staring at the door feeling too nervous to knock and ask to see Jeremy Brown, the Chair-rat.

'Oh well, Hastings House, here we come...' announces Roger.

Whether it is a sudden burst of courage or a sudden moment of impatience will never be known but without warning Brian knocks on the round wooden door of Hastings House. Tap! Tap! Tap! The door echoes in the darkness as Brian knocks loudly and firmly.

The Door opens...

The two friends stare silently at each other in a mixture of surprise and wonder. Even Brian is surprised and even a little shocked at his own actions and now they wonder what will happen to them. They do not wait long to find out. They barely draw breath when the door quickly opens.

'Oh, it's you two again,' says the big guard.

The big guard is standing behind the door that he has opened only slightly. It is just enough of a gap to see through and he is peering through making sure there is definitely not enough of a gap to pass either in or out Though hiding behind the door he is still wearing his uniform and helmet, the two friends can just about see this.

'Oh, there you are,' responds Brian.

'Yes, it's us,' Roger replies, feeling guilty.

Roger wonders if the grumpy guard overheard their words from behind the round wooden door, he certainly opened it quickly. Brian, however, does not share his friend's concerns.

'What happened? You get lonely outside?' Brian asks cheekily.

'Can we come in? We've come to see...'

'I know why you are here,' the guard answers, bluntly.

The guard rudely interrupts Roger not allowing him to finish his question, he does not even look at him, instead he stares at the little statue of Nelson's Column. However neither

Roger nor Brian are too bothered because this time the guard lets them in without much fuss.

Struggling, the two friends awkwardly carry the ornament through the doorway into Hastings House while the big guard stands holding the door watching impatiently. Once again they find themselves in the big square room with the fitted red carpet and like before they make their way as quietly as possible to the desk at the other end of the room. Here, also like before, the grey furred middle-aged female rat is sitting quietly working and again she is dressed in a grey skirt and jacket. Both Roger and Brian cannot help but wonder if this stern-looking rat which reminds them of a schoolteacher has been sitting here ever since their first visit. She certainly looks the same as before.

The two friends hear the door shut behind them and looking round they see the grumpy guard sitting down staring moodily at them with his furry arms folded. They ignore him and return their attention to the grey female rat.

'Excuse me,' asks Roger, quietly.

It is extremely quiet in this room, the only sound that can be heard is of water gently dripping somewhere. This silence along with the lack of friendliness makes poor Roger and Brian feel awkward.

The female rat does not appear to have heard or even noticed their arrival.

'Excuse me,' repeats Roger, quietly again.

This time the grey female rat looks up. Without speaking she looks up at Roger, then she looks at Brian. Next she takes a long hard look at the little ornament of Nelson's Column which stands between the two friends. Finally she returns her gaze onto Roger.

'Yes?' she asks.

'Um, we've come to see the Chair-rat,' explains Roger.

'He should be expecting us,' adds Brian.

He adds this trying to be helpful, but wonders if instead it sounds rude.

'Should he?' she asks.

'Yes, he should,' Brian responds.

Brian has been standing feeling quite out of place coping with bad manners and all this after a long journey. Now he is beginning to feel quite angry and does not mind anyone knowing this but before anything else can be said another rat appears. It is the old broad rat in the long black coat and grey pin-striped trousers with the whiskery grey head above the stiff white collar.

'This way,' he says calmly.

Roger and Brian quickly pick up their ornament once more and find themselves following this rat's well-dressed tail. This time he leads them straight into the Chair-rat's office without knocking and without leaving them in the viewing gallery staring at buses.

'Roger and Brian to see you sir.'

He remembers their names, this impresses the two friends very much and they look up at him only to see his face hidden in a shadow. They still do not know what he looks like.

Jeremy Brown the Chair-rat of the Rats Underground Southwest Drains Region quickly takes his hairy bare feet off his desk and sits up in his chair.

'Ah! Um... Yes?' he says.

Roger and Brian put their ornament down once more and stand looking at their Chair-rat in his office while catching their breath. For some reason the first thing they notice is the chair in which Jeremy Brown is sitting, it is an old egg cup with a side removed and converted very neatly into a very comfortable seat. It certainly looks comfortable the way the Chair-rat swivels and slouches, it must be comfortable. Even at his desk which they observe next is made from plywood with panels covering the front and the sides that hide the Chair-rat's legs from view which is probably why they never noticed his egg cup chair before. What the two friends noticed on their first visit to Jeremy Brown's nice office and are enjoying now is the soft fitted red carpet under their hairy bare feet.

But for Roger and Brian the most important thing in this room is the very grand full length painting on the wall behind the Chair-rat Jeremy Brown. It is, as they remember a painting of Nelson Brown, the ancestor of Jeremy Brown. After all the rat in the long bushy white wig and fancy clothing in the picture is the reason why Roger and Brian have been on their quest. If it was not for the pride Jeremy Brown feels for his ancestor who was a co-founder of the Rats Underground they would not have been to London and back. Now they are standing either side of the ornament of Nelson's Column waiting to give it to the Chair-rat and hopefully go home.

Suddenly and quite worryingly the two friends realize how different the painting and their ornament look. Their ornament is of a man with one arm and leaning on a sword. He is wearing a long frock coat, open at the legs. On his chest are medals and on his shoulders are epaulettes which are frilly shoulder pads. On his head is not a wig but a big flat wide hat with a rosette. Clearly this man is nothing like the rat in the painting.

'Roger and Brian? Who are they?' asks the Chair-rat.

This makes the two friends jump as they were both daydreaming and wondering how long this is going to take before they can go home.

'Roger and Brian sir are the two you sent for the statue of Nelson,' the butler explains.

'Statue? Roger and Brian..? Ah! Roger and Brian! Yes! Still no uniform...' he observes eventually.

Roger and Brian do not say a word, instead they just stand in silence staring at their absent-minded Chair-rat wearing his tight and ill fitting grey suit.

Finally the Chair-rat pays them enough attention to realize they have brought something with them.

'What is that?' he asks pointing at the ornament.

'It's the statue you ordered,' answers Roger.

'Sir,' adds Brian.

'Did I? Oh yes, I did... Is it?' replies the Chair-rat.

He stares long and hard at the ornament of Nelson's Column. The two friends have the uneasy feeling that he realizes that it looks nothing like the rat in the painting. This though after a thought Roger considers obvious, after all there are no famous statues of rats anywhere. Roger knows that rats are not usually popular with people, but despite this he senses the Chair-rat is still not pleased.

'It's Nelson's Column,' explains Roger.

'Is it?' asks the Chair-rat, coolly.

'It's a famous landmark,' adds Roger.

'Is it?' asks the Chair-rat.

This time he sounds a little more interested. He glances quickly over his shoulder at the painting but eventually returns his attention to the statue.

'Yes, from London, the capital of England and all that,' Brian adds.

Brian also senses the Chair-rat is a little less than pleased and joins in with Roger's attempt to be impressive. Neither can bear to think what might happen if their Chair-rat is not happy with the ornament so together they behave with enthusiasm.

'From London? I've been there once. Has anyone noticed that it's missing? Are they looking for it?' asks the Chair-rat.

'Oh it's not the real one!' Brian blurts out.

Brian regrets his words the moment he has said them, but it is always too late by then.

'You mean it's a copy?' the Chair-rat questions them.

Disappointment and even frustration can be heard in his voice, the two friends are worried now. They just wanted to deliver the statue and go home but instead here they are in this important rat's office answering his questions.

'Well… Um...' mutters Brian.

'The original is almost one hundred metres tall,' explains Roger, thinking quickly.

'Oh, I see… A bit too big then. Never fit it into the R.U.,' accepts the Chair-rat.

'No, wouldn't fit on the train either,' adds Brian.

'Train?'

'Yes, it's how we got to London and back,' explains Roger.

'Ah, train, yes… Good idea!' the Chair-rat praises.

For the first time since they had arrived in Hastings House, Roger and Brian feel pleased. They are both pleasantly surprised, so far the Chair-rat has not been either especially friendly, nor has he seemed very interested in them. Nor for that matter has any other rat in Hastings House been very warm and friendly towards them. But now to their relief and delight their Chair-rat shows some appreciation of their effort.

'Anyway, thank you both very much. Thank you, um… Roger and Brian. Oh yes and take the day off,' the grateful Chair-rat says.

Roger and Brian are pleased and even pleasantly surprised, relieved even. Not only does the Chair-rat seem happy with their weekend of work but he has given them the day off. Normally Roger and Brian spend their Monday's having to work on the Rats Underground clearing blockages. This is a very dirty, smelly job which today they can happily avoid, instead they can stay nice and clean doing whatever they choose.

The two friends realize the Chair-rat is finally happy with the statue they have got for him and sense that now at last he has finished with them. Seizing the opportunity Roger and Brian hastily leave his office.

And so to Bed...

It is as though visiting Jeremy Brown, the Chair-rat of the Rats Underground Southwest Drains Region in his very nice office in Hastings House never happened. Twice they have stood on his soft red carpet in the head office and the first time a Herald summoned them to see the Chair-rat himself! Now quite suddenly they find themselves standing outside the round wooden door which was closed very quickly when they stepped outside. But it all did happen including the good fun they had in London.

Once more the two friends find themselves all alone as they stand on the cold hard concrete in the gloom of the R.U. They stare at their moored boat which is tied up safely as it gently floats in the murky water. After a weekend of adventure away from home this is a pleasant sight to them, it is a sight inviting them home to bed, food and relaxing.

'Well…' remarks Roger.

'Yes, well,' agrees Brian.

'Our time is our own,' Roger observes.

'Once again,' notes Brian.

'At last!' Roger sighs.

After an unexpected and rather busy weekend away from home the two friends are just so glad to be back in their home town. For a few moments Roger and Brian look at their boat while listening to the sound of water gently flowing in the quietness of this stretch of the Rats Underground. It is peaceful, safe and they live here, very happily.

'Well,' repeats Roger.

'I'm hungry,' admits Brian.

Brian's hunger gives Roger an idea, a simple idea but an idea all the same, one that can take advantage of their extra free time.

'I know, lets go for a picnic,' he suggests.

'I'd like to go home, Rog,' Brian admits, honestly.

'Well, let's get a picnic we can enjoy at home,' Roger replies.

Roger is neither upset nor put off by his friend's desire to go home. Roger also longs to be home yet at the same time he wishes to enjoy their free day. Brian though is hungry and wisely decides that Roger's second suggestion would be fun and practical and after a pause agrees;

'Ok, a picnic we can take home.'

The two friends are happy, their adventure might be over but so to is their job, task or even quest for the column and now once again their time is their own. With this thought in mind Roger and Brian climb into their boat chatting away cheerfully.

'You can row Rog.'

'I always row,' says Roger.

'Yeah, well you're getting good at it,' answers Brian.

'Oh, thanks... What do you mean "getting"?' asks Roger.

'Well practice makes perfect,' explains Brian.

And when do you practice?' Roger asks.

'Ah... Um... Well I don't want to stop an expert like you from honing your skills, you're very good!' Brian replies.

'I am, aren't I?' agrees Roger.

Roger and Brian's boat slowly fades away into the gloomy tunnel of the Rats Underground. Their voices become more faint as they disappear into the distance as the sight of the little old fruit bowl of a boat with wooden spoons for oars is steadily rowed through the murky water.

'Well that's one adventure over and done with Brian.'

'Yeah, I wonder what next?' he replies.